FAITHFUL WIFE'S FA
BOOK
PETE ANDREWS

ABOUT THE AUTHOR

I write sexy romances. I used to publish under *xleglover* and *Flash of Stocking* on various sites.

My stories are romances, so they delve into the feelings, emotions and relationships of the characters. My stories are also erotica, so the sex scenes are explicit. Often *very* explicit.

My stories have an emotional edge to them. The characters have thrilling adventures, but there's pain there too, at least for some of them.

I try to write stories that seem like real life. Yes, the situations are extreme, but I hope you come away thinking, "*Yes, I can see how that might happened.*"

You can find my books on sites like *Amazon Kindle* and *Smashwords*. Also *Barnes & Noble, Apple Books,* and *Rakuten kobo*. If you'd like to join my mailing list or would like to send me a question or feedback, please email me at *peteandrews1701@gmail.com*.

BOOKS BY PETE ANDREWS

Faithful Wife's Fall From Grace (on-going series)

Book 1
Book 2
Book 3
Book 4

Girls Who Belong To Other Men (2 book series)

Book 1
Book 2

Opening Pandora's Box (5 book series)

Book 1: Jessie Plays For Her Husband
Book 2: Ollie Watches His Wife With Another Man
Book 3: Jessie Grows Closer To Roman
Book 4: Jessie Loses Herself In Roman
Book 5: How Can You Do This To Me?

Available at Amazon Kindle and Smashwords.

CHAPTER 1

I woke to the sounds of the house coming alive. People were stirring. I heard plates and pots clanking around from early risers making breakfast in the kitchen.

I realized 2 things immediately. I was alone in the cot. And I was hungover. I guess that was no surprise as I hadn't drunk that much and smoked weed in a long time.

I pulled myself from the cot and made my way to the kitchen. Jen was there, along with Allie and a few others. To my relief Scott wasn't there.

Jen looked bright and cheerful. How was that possible after all the drinking last night? She had even showered and changed into a black, long sleeve top and black North Face ski tights. Her lush, wavy blonde hair was brushed into a silky luster. She even had a little lipstick on. She looked all ready for a day on the slopes.

Allie grinned and said, "God Mike you look like shit," and that set off a few good natured chuckles.

Jen brought me a cup of coffee, looking at me with an apprehensive smile. "Morning sleepy head," she said with a kiss to my cheek. I desperately needed to talk to her. I motioned to the hallway, and she nodded, and we moved there.

"What happened last night?" I asked.

A couple walked by and we said polite good mornings. Other people were waking up. Jen whispered "It's too crowded to talk."

"Then when?"

"I don't know. Later."

"What are you doing today?" I asked.

"Scott and I are about to go skiing," Jen said.

My eyes opened wide, and my jaw dropped. "You're going without me?" I said shocked.

"He's teaching me to ski," Jen said.

"You talked to him already?"

She gave me a look, as if saying "what, talking is a crime?" Then she said, "He's in the locker room with the other guys getting things ready."

I stared at her. I couldn't believe it. She got up early and left me alone in the cot. She showered and dressed. She made plans with her "best bud." And now she was about to leave me for the day. And this was AFTER she got fingered by the man she was going skiing with! And what else happened after I passed out?!

Jen was so enamored and in heat over Scott she was forgetting all about me! I felt incredibly jealous and hurt!

And the way she said it—"he's in the locker room with the *other guys*." What, I'm not one of the guys anymore?

"You can go if you want but I didn't think you'd want to," Jen said filling the silence. "You don't like Scott."

Her half-hearted offer was like a punch to the gut. More people walked by and we had to stop talking. We made polite small talk until they moved on to the kitchen. We needed more privacy. I pulled Jen into a bathroom down the hall.

"I can't believe you're going skiing alone with Scott," I hissed in a low voice.

"I'm not going alone. Other people will be there," she whispered back.

"But you'll be with Scott!" I said, exasperation creeping into my voice.

"Calm down Mike. People know we're friends," she said calmly. How could she be so calm? Her dismissive tone cut at my gut. How could she not see how this was making me feel?

"You don't think they won't notice you're going with Scott and leaving me here?" I shot back.

Jen frowned at me, and was silent a moment, as if counting to 10. Then she said, "What do you want me to do Mike? I'm mean, I thought that's what I'm supposed to do. Flirt with Scott. That's our game, right? I can't flirt with Scott if I'm not with him."

There it was. She threw it back into my court. I was the one pushing her to play our "game." I was the one telling her it was okay to be "buds" with Scott and spend time with him. I was the one encouraging her to go to happy hours and lunches with Scott. I was the one giving her space yesterday so she could do whatever with Scott.

And now she was annoyed I was pulling back. I was changing the rules of the game. I was reverting back to the old "I get insanely jealous if another man looks at you" Mike.

"We always said we'd stop if either of us said so," I said, reminding her of the rules we talked about before. Veto power was one of them. The other big one was if she felt like she was getting emotionally attached, she had to tell me immediately so we could deal with it.

"I know," she agreed. "Are you saying stop?"

I hesitated. I knew if I stopped it now, Jen would probably never play again. My fantasies would remain just that. Fantasies. We were young. We didn't have kids yet. This was probably the only time in our lives we could experiment like this.

"I'm not saying that," I finally said, relenting. "I'm just saying ... this is hard for me."

Jen softened. She smiled and rubbed my chest. She explained, "I barely talked to Scott this morning. The group planned it a long time ago. We're doing all the black diamonds today. I'm not going because of Scott. I'm going because they are all really good skiers and I want to get better. I didn't think you'd want to go because you're not that into skiing. And Scott's a real ass sometimes and you don't like him, so I didn't want you to have to deal with that. So I was actually thinking about you, and looking out for you."

I nodded slowly. What she said *did* made me feel better. But Jen's a marketing chick and she's good at her job. She knows the right words to say to sell things.

Again, I wanted to ask what happened last night. About what happened in the pool room. How far it went. But I knew that conversation would take a lot of time and Jen looked like she was in a hurry to get back to the group. "What's the rush?" I asked.

"The skiing's better on the south facing slopes before noon," she said. I paused, processing that information. Jen wasn't a ski bum, so how did she know that? From Scott? Jealousy flared in me.

Jen read my mind. "RH told me that," she said.

I raised my eyebrows, surprised. "He's here?" I asked.

"He got here last night."

Last night. I wondered when. Before or after Jen got fingered?

I was glad RH was here. We were friends, so at least I had one ally in the house.

"He's back together with Allie?" I asked.

"They're supposed to be," Jen said with a shrug. "I don't know. I don't think they know."

I was silent for a moment, processing that. Allie wasn't my favorite person, but I didn't wish any harm to her. I remembered how scared and vulnerable she looked last night. Was Allie really a frightened little girl behind all that sassy Oh-La-La confidence?

"I'm sorry I bailed on you last night," Jen said, putting her palm on my stomach. "I drank so much and we passed around joints."

"What time was it? When you got into the cot with me?" I asked.

"I don't know," she said with a helpless laugh. She rubbed my arm and said, "Grace told me you did a liquor run last night. A mile and back in the snow. Now she thinks you walk on water. You're freaking awesome Mike." She smiled into my eyes. I couldn't help smiling back. Still though, her praise felt bittersweet since I knew she was about to spend the day with Scott. "I'm sorry I didn't take care of this last night," she said, putting her hand on my crotch.

Jen got on her knees. She unbuckled my pants and pulled down the zipper, then she took my cock out. I was already hard. She swallowed me, holding my shaft at the base with one hand and caressing my balls with her other. I loved it when she lightly scratched her manicured nails along the underside of my balls. God it felt so good!

My head rolled back as she licked and sucked me. I instinctively grabbed her head with both hands.

Jen pulled away and looked up at me. "Mike baby?" she said.

"Yeah, what?" I asked, breathing hard and panting.

"Don't mess up my hair, okay baby?" she said.

I looked at her. I got it. She'd spent time doing her hair. She wanted to look pretty. For Scott.

I nodded and took my hands off her head. She went back down on me, and I clenched the edge of the counter.

Afterwards Jen brushed her teeth with a little toothpaste on her finger, and swished mouth wash through her mouth. She saw me watching her. "Sorry, I just don't want cum breath around everyone," she said.

I nodded. I understood, but now I really felt she had gone down on me just to appease me, so I'd give her room to spend more time with Scott.

———————⟶●⟵———————

Everyone headed off into groups. I went skiing on my own. It was okay. I liked being alone.

I'd skied a couple times before. To be honest I'm not that good. I think I *could* get good if I tried. I was like that in all sports. If I tried I could get good. Not professional good, but decent. But I'm a thinker, that's what I'm good at. Math and computers. Like the Sapphire project at work.

Still, I have pride like any other guy. So I worked really hard at skiing today. I started with the Greens to get my ski legs back. Then I did all the Blues. I tried a Black. Well, that was ugly. Can you say *yard sale*? I went back to the Blues. I did all of them again. Then I went back to that Black. I did it! Then I did another. Success!

I stayed clear of the double black diamonds. I mean, I'm not crazy. The point is, in just a day, I got decent at skiing. I knew Scott was a college skier, he had a scholarship. Well, maybe if I skied as much as him, I could've gotten a scholarship too. But could Scott have gotten a scholarship in math? Could he have gotten a PhD in math and CS? Could he have won the Barnes award? I doubted it.

I purposefully stayed late on the slopes, until it got almost dark and the slopes were mostly empty. Partly it was because I was having fun. But also, I wanted Jen to worry about me. I wanted her to worry that maybe I got hurt. So then she'd feel guilty about leaving me alone. I knew it was childish but it felt good.

The prank worked too because when I got to the house Jen was looking concerned, talking worriedly with Allie and Grace in the kitchen. When she saw me, she rushed to me, looking incredibly relieved. When she asked why I was home so late, I just brushed it off with a shrug and nonchalantly told her I wanted to do another run down a black.

Holding my arm, she gave me a crooked grin and said, "So this is you punishing me, right?"

I knew I was busted but I managed to keep a straight face as I innocently said, "Punish you? About what?"

Jen laughed. "Come on," she said as she led me into the big common room.

The common room had a huge fireplace in the middle surrounded by sofas, chairs and pillows. The room was lit only by the fireplace, and there was Trance music in the background, so it had a mellow New York clubby vibe to it. It seemed like everyone was there, talking and laughing and drinking whatever. Joints were being passed around. The party looked like a continuation of last night.

I saw Scott. There was an empty seat next to him. Every other spot was taken up, but it was empty next to him. I realized that Jen had been sitting there, next to Scott, before talking to Allie and Grace in the kitchen.

Jen was considerate enough to my feelings not to sit next to Scott again. She sat a few people over, and people moved to make room for us. One of my Highland Park bottles was on the coffee table. Jen poured a generous amount into a tumbler with a couple cubes of ice and handed it to me. "What, are you trying to get me drunk?" I joked, looking at the double pour in the glass.

"I just want you to relax baby," she told me, rubbing my shoulder. "Anyways, you need to catch up."

When she passed me a joint a few minutes later, I wondered if she was hoping I would pass out so she could be with Scott again.

Someone was mixing vodka cocktails. Scott said, "I'll have one, shaken not stirred." Jen (and a few others) laughed at his predictable James Bond joke.

"You know that was an intentional joke," I said.

"What?" Scott said, not understanding me. Now everyone in the room was listening.

"When you shake vodka in ice, all you get is watery vodka," I said. "Ian Fleming knew that. He wrote it into the James Bond books as an inside joke."

Scott scowled at me, realizing *he* was now the butt of the joke by repeating the James Bond line. Actually, I had no idea if what I said was true or not. That made my little victory even sweeter.

My victory was short-lived though because Jen leaned over and whispered, "Be nice Mike." I looked at her, frowning. What, he can diss me, but I can't diss him? And then I saw it. She had her cum face on.

I guess I didn't see it before. Or maybe her lust had taken a momentary back seat to her concern for me. But now it was definitely there. Her cum face.

When Jen was aroused, she always had a certain, longing look on her pretty face. Her cheeks got flushed. Her eyes became heavy-lidded. Her lips often parted slightly, like she was breathing hard.

Jen always got that look when she was sexually excited. It was her tell. I called it her *cum face*.

Jen had her cum face on now. So I knew she was sexually aroused. And I knew Scott got her that way, not me.

For the first time that evening, I looked at what she was wearing. A loose green turtleneck and mini-skirt. Black tights, and her black pointy toe Mia flats, the ones with black silk ribbons that wrapped mid-way up her shapely calves. Her long blonde hair was down, and she had it back with a silk-covered hair band that matched the green of her turtle neck. She looked cute and sexy at the same time.

Then, I noticed 2 things and it made me catch my breath. First, while the turtleneck was loose, it kind of clung to her breasts. The natural shape of her breasts were outlined by the shirt, and her perky upturned nipples dented the soft cotton fabric. Jen wasn't wearing a bra.

And when I looked down at her legs, just below her skirt, I briefly saw a flash of soft skin before she adjusted and pulled down her skirt. She was wearing the kind of tights that ended up her thighs, like thigh high stockings.

People started gathering into small groups and spreading out through the house, like last night. "I'm going to talk to Scotty," she whispered to me. She looked at me, as if waiting for me to object and say no.

I shrugged and nodded my head. I tried to act like I didn't care. But I cared. It felt like a knife was in my heart.

Jen moved over to join Scott's circle. She held my hand so I followed. They started up again. Laughing and talking. Jen touching him as she talked with her hands. Smiling up into his face. She rarely looked at me, or tried to bring me into the conversation. I felt like a forgotten third wheel.

Was I turned on? Yes, I was so hard it hurt. Everything I read about cuckold fantasies was coming true. The physical part – the actual sex – that wasn't the hard part. It was the emotions that were hard. Like Jen wanting to be with Scott. Her face lighting up when he walked into the room. The way she hung on his every word, and laughed at all his jokes. The way she seemed so infatuated with him.

Jen passed me the joint a few times. I sucked in the weed between sips of the Highland Park. I grabbed the bottle and topped off my glass. I went along with what Jen wanted. I got drunk and high.

I wandered off and lost sight of Jen and Scott. Or maybe they wandered off.

People started having sex. Not an orgy or mate swapping. Just couples pairing up. Married couples. Boyfriends with their girlfriends. The singles too, eyeing potential new significant others, pairing up and having sex.

People went into bedrooms but there weren't enough of those to go around. So they found semi-private places to fuck. The sex was all around but you averted your eyes out of politeness.

I staggered around, scotch in one hand and joint in the other. I was trying to find Jen. I feared the worst. But I needed to find her.

At one point I looked into a bedroom. Allie and RH were there. They were naked on the bed, and Allie was on top riding RH. Allie was facing the door. Her breasts were incredible. I preferred tiny tits like Jen's, but Allie's big ones were about the most perfect you would ever see. It was the first time I ever saw Allie nude. And also the first time I saw her getting fucked.

Allie had her eyes closed as she rode RH. Then she opened her eyes and looked at me. I expected one of those derisive, sassy Allie smiles, but instead it was a friendly smile, like she was saying "you can stay and watch if you want."

So I stayed and watched from the doorway. I watched Allie cum. It was a beautiful sight, watching Allie's face as she orgasmed.

I didn't wait around to see RH finish. Instead, I staggered down the hall. It was stupid getting so drunk and high. Maybe this was the only way I could deal with it. I had become obsessed with Jen with another man. But I was afraid too, so maybe this was the only way I could deal with it. The only way I could let it happen.

I kept walking through the house, stumbling sometimes, looking for Jen. Where were they? Then I saw the fireplace room was crowded again. It seemed like everyone was there. Even Allie and RH (who had gotten dressed again after their quickie). That's when I saw Jen.

CHAPTER 2

Flashback – Last Night and the Next Morning
   "So where's hubby?" Scott said as I joined him by the bonfire.
   "He's hanging," I said.

   "You gave him the joint?"

   I frowned and instantly regretted telling Scott about how Mike used to get salty when I talked to other guys. "Scotty, don't tell him I told you that," I said. "I'll get in so much trouble if he finds out you told me to give him the joint so he'll chill. You can be a major ass sometimes. So don't say anything."

   "Okay, I'll be good," Scott promised, giving me an innocent *"who me?"* look. "I'll try to be just a minor ass."

   "Gawd," I said, laughing and punching his arm at his stupid joke.

   "You ready for the black diamonds tomorrow?" he said grinning at me.

   "You getcha mister," I said, grinning back at him.

   "I'm looking forward to seeing you in tight ski pants," Scott said grinning at me.

   I gave him an innocent look and said "I was supposed to bring pants? Well darn. All I have are tights. I hope they're warm enough as I'll just have a black lacy thong underneath."

   Scott laughed and said, "God Jen. You know you're fucking killing me?"

   "Killing you, how?" I asked with that innocent voice again.

   Scott laughed again.

   That's how it was with me and Scott. We flirted all the time. But it was just messing around. I was JenJen again, and that was what

JenJen did, she flirted with boys. But it didn't mean anything. It was all harmless. After all, I was happily married.

At least, that's what I told myself. And when I told myself this, I tried not to think about what I'd done with Joey. What I was *doing* with Joey.

Bobby ran out of firewood, so the party moved back inside. I looked around for Mike. Then Grace told me he went on a liquor run, gushing about how great a guy he was. That didn't surprise me. Mike *was* a great guy.

Scott said something to Bobby. Then Bobby turned down the lights in the big fireplace room and put on Trance music. Now the big room was dark except for the flickering embers of the fireplace. For a while we clustered in groups, drinking beer and smoking weed as we talked in low voices and gently swayed to the beat of the sexy Trance music.

Ian Van Dahl's version of "Will I?" started playing. It was a fast song and some people picked up the beat. Me and Scott though, we chilled through the song, swaying with every third beat while standing in place and talking.

I felt hands on my ass. Different hands. Guys were talking advantage of the dark and the close confides and checking me out.

I wondered who was touching me. Most of the people there were from work. Not everyone was the same level. Me and Allie were the same, both account execs. There were a few partners there, mostly newly minted like Scott. And also people more junior.

Like, there were a couple guys there, Vince and Steve, and they actually worked for me. I was their boss. Had they copped a feel? I wasn't sure how I felt about that. Monday might be awkward at work. But it was crowded, people were standing close together, I couldn't do anything about it without making a scene.

People started dancing. It was more like couples with arms around each other swaying in place to the music. Scott pulled me into his arms.

We often danced at happy hours – I danced with a lot of guys – so this was no big deal. Scotty held me tight, so tight I felt his erection against my leg. I kicked off the UGGs to make it easier to dance.

"This is hot," Scott whispered to me.

"What?" I asked, not sure if he was talking about me, or the scene, or the Trace beats.

"This," he said, touching my wool cable knit sweater.

Without asking, he took hold of the bottom and pulled up. Without thinking I held up my arms and he pulled it off me. Underneath I was only wearing a chemise. It was off-white and made of silk. I was braless underneath.

"Much better," Scott said, his hands on my back. His hands were partly on the silk of the chemise, and partly on my bare skin above the chemise.

"Scott, are you freaking crazy?" I asked, feeling exposed in the flimsy chemise. The chemise was almost see through and my nipples easily dented the delicate fabric.

"Chill Jen, I know you like guys looking," Scott said.

"What?"

"You've got the innocent act going, but you're really a cock tease," Scott said. "I know what you're into."

I pulled back from Scott and looked into his face. "And what am I into Scott?" I asked putting as much icy contempt into my voice as possible.

Scott grinned at me. Then he leaned close to my ear and whispered, "You're a submissive slut and you want to be bent over a table and fucked in the ass."

My lips parted into an O. I tried to hide it but Scott was still holding me, so he felt my body tense. He grinned at me again, knowing he had discovered my secret.

"I'm not into that," I said, pushing away from him.

"Yeah right," he said sarcastically, still grinning.

"No seriously. I don't like it up the ass," I deadpanned. I tried to make a joke out of it, and Scott laughed, but still we both knew the truth.

Scott knew my secret. In real life, I tried to be a strong woman. A feminist. But when it came to sex, I was submissive. At least, that's what I fantasized about. I fantasized about being controlled and dominated by a strong man. About being treated like an object. About being used.

I wasn't into getting tied up or whipped. Although sometimes in my fantasy, the man holds me down. I resist but he's big and strong and I can't move. I don't want to like it, but he forces me to like it. My body betrays me. I try not to cum but he forces me to cum. That's the part that really drives me wild. Just thinking the words gets me hot.

He forces me to cum.

Somehow Scott and I ended up in the empty game room downstairs. Along the way I had a couple more beers and another joint as we chatted with people. I definitely felt high and tipsy.

The room was spinning and I put my hands on the edge of the pool table for balance. "Are you okay?" Scott asked, rubbing my back. If he didn't already know I was braless, he found out then. I was still only wearing the chemise so it practically felt like his hand was on my bare skin.

"Just give me a sec," I said. Now in addition to the room spinning, my skin was tingling with his hands on me.

"Come here, I'll help you," Scott said. He leaned against the pool table and pulled me into his arms.

"This is helping me?" I asked with a helpless laugh.

Then Scott's lips were on mine. I was surprised and tensed up for a moment. Then I gave into it. Scott was a really good kisser. A freaking awesome kisser.

Finally, I pushed him away. We were both panting.

"Scotty, we can't be doing this," I said between pants, looking warily at him.

"I think it's about time we're doing this," he said.

Scott's arms were still around me. He caressed my back, almost down to my ass. Then he began inching his hands up under my chemise. He was now caressing the bare skin of my back. As his hands moved up my back – now he was touching the middle of my back, where my bra strap would be if I had worn a bra – the entire chemise moved up, so my breasts were almost exposed.

"Scotty, Mike's upstairs," I said, my heart racing.

"He's probably still on the liquor run."

"He might be back by now."

Scott ignored my words. He didn't care if Mike was upstairs. He looked down at my chest. If my nipples were hard before, they were like diamonds now. They dented the silk of the chemise, and you could just make out the dark of my areolas through the delicate fabric.

"You do more with less than anyone I know," he said, his eyes on my bust.

"I guess that's a compliment," I said with another helpless laugh.

Scott grinned at me. He reached between our bodies and cupped one of my breasts with his hand. He gave it a squeeze, then thumbed my nipple over the chemise.

"Scott, Mike's upstairs," I whispered desperately.

He ignored me. He continued to fondle my breast and rub my nipple. The feel of his thumb over the silk felt so good. I started breathing heavier, and a moan escaped my lips.

"Tiny tits, sensitive nipples, right?" he said giving me a knowing smile. He'd been with enough girls to know the two usually went together.

"Scott, you need to stop," I said breathlessly, the words coming out like a moan. My eyelids fluttered and I rolled my head back.

With his other hand on my back, he pulled me closer so I felt his erection against my stomach. "This is what you do to me," he said, grinding his erection against me. "You've been doing this to me for weeks. Months. You little cock tease."

"Scotty ...."

Then he kissed me again. I kissed him back. Our tongues danced in our mouths. His hands were all over me. Then he got my shorts open and pushed his hand down my tights and panties. I didn't resist. I parted my legs to give him better access.

He pushed one finger into me. Then another. "Oh god," I groaned.

I heard him hiss "you're so wet!" Then he was finger fucking me and rubbing my clit with his thumb. I moaned and pushed down against his hand. Trying to stop what was happening.

But Scott wouldn't stop. His fingers and thumb were relentless. He pushed so deep into me, he lifted me onto my tiptoes. I had to hold onto his arms for balance. I wimped and moaned into his mouth as he made me cum. I clung to his arms as my body shuddered and shook with orgasmic pleasure.

Scotty held me as I caught my breath. Then he kissed me again. Scott pulled my shorts the rest of the way off, and began tugging down my tights. Finally, I pushed away from him. "No Scott, please, Mike ...." I said.

He wasn't happy about it. I was leaving him with major blue balls. But to his credit he stopped when he heard me really say no.

I pulled up my tights and shorts and ran from the room. I found my sweater and put it back on. I looked into the family room with the cots. Mike was there. It looked like he was sleeping. Or maybe not. But I wasn't ready to join him, not after what just happened with Scott.

People were in the kitchen. Allie and a few others, and RH finally arrived. We drank beers and passed around another joint. It helped me calm down. Scott walked in and sat at the table across from me. He was frowning at me. I knew he was pissed. But what could I do? I was married.

Again, I tried not to think about Joey.

Finally, I went to the cot room. I was high and half drunk. God, when was the last time I drunk so much, and smoked so much weed? College? I got into the cot with Mike and got him to spoon me. Almost immediately I passed out.

The next morning, I woke up to a shake of my shoulder. I opened my eyes. It was Scott. "Wheels up in an hour," he told me tersely. "Me and the guys are getting the gear ready." I could tell he was still pissed about last night. I just nodded. He looked at Mike and frowned.

I looked over my shoulder at Mike. He was still asleep. He was snuggled into my back with his arm around me. What, Scott didn't like the way we slept? He was my freaking husband for god's sake.

Being careful not to wake Mike, I got out of the cot. I realized my shorts were off. I was naked from the waist down, other than the black tights. Scott's eyes were on me. I let him look. In fact, I liked him looking at me. I grabbed my bag and went to the bathroom, pushing passed Scott without saying a word to him. If he was going to be a shit about last night, then I could be a shit too.

I got in the shower. Fortunately there were a lot of bathrooms in the house and it was early so there was no waiting. I was surprised how good I was feeling after all the partying last night. I seemed to remember Mike making me drink a glass of water and take Advil. It made me smile. Mike always took care of me.

As I washed my nipples and pussy, I realized I was horny. Super horny. My body was on fire. Without even thinking, I began playing with myself, one hand on my breasts, the other on my clit. As the shower rained down on me, I found myself with my face pressed against the ceramic tile. I was on my tiptoes, my eyes clenched shut, as I squeezed my nipples with one hand and rapidly stroked my clit with the other. I fantasized about Scott pushing me over the pool table and fucking me from behind. *Forcing me* from behind. When I came I bit my lip to keep from moaning (I didn't want anyone passing in the hall to hear me). As my breathing returned to normal, I realized that wasn't enough. I needed something inside me. Not just anyone. I wanted Scott.

After doing my hair and dressing, I checked on Mike. He was still sleeping. I sat next to him for a few moments, gently stroking his hair. I loved him so much. Yet I was cheating on him with Joey. And now I wanted sex with Scott. I used to be such a prim and proper wife. A faithful wife. Things had changed so fast. So much for my marriage vows. I waited for the guilt to come but it didn't. Maybe because I wanted Scott so much and that was pushing away the guilt. Or maybe because it was this "game" we were playing. Mike had opened a Pandora's box and I kinda felt like that gave me an excuse.

I went into the kitchen and helped with breakfast. A little while later Mike walked in, looking sleepy and hungover. I smiled at him and brought him a cup of coffee. I kissed him on the cheek. "Morning sleepy head," I said smiling at him.

But I was nervous. I spent most of yesterday with Scott and I could tell Mike was upset. And there was what happened last night in the game room. Did he have any clue? Did someone see us and tell him? I didn't want a major scene. For one we were around co-workers and drama between us wouldn't be good. But also I wanted to spend time with Scott today; I didn't want Mike to say no.

I know that sounds terrible. But I was feeling defensive about it all. I mean, this was *our* game. It wasn't just me. It was both of us.

Mike wanted to see me with another man. Well, *hello*, the only way to do that was to *be with* the other man. And if you put a boy and a girl together, sometimes things happen. Mike had woken up something inside me. Did it make me a terrible person to want to see it through?

Mike motioned to the hallway and we moved there.

"What happened last night?" he asked.

A couple walked by and we said polite good mornings. Other people were waking up. I whispered "It's too crowded to talk."

"Then when?"

"I don't know. Later."

[Author's note: See above for the rest of Mike and Jen's conversation.]

———————◈———————

The house was ski-on / ski-off, so we skated on our skis to the first lift. There were 14 of us, a perfect number to share the 2 person lifts. Throughout the day people changed lift partners but I mostly rode with Scott. People knew we were buddies so no one tried to cut into our pairing. Looking back, there were probably rumors flying around about me and Scott, but at the time I was oblivious to it.

I was glad Mike wasn't with us. Don't judge me too harshly, as it was mostly because I didn't want him to get hurt. Mike wasn't an experienced skier, but he's stubborn and determined, so I knew he'd want to try everything especially with Scotty there. Our plan was to do all the blacks and some had nasty moguls, and I didn't want Mike to get hurt.

But, to be fair, I admit it was also because of Scott. This way I got to ride with him on lifts and hang with him.

It wasn't all flirting. I really did want to get better. Scotty's an awesome skier and he took me under his wing. On the lift rides we spent a lot of time talking about the last run, what I did wrong, what I could do different next time. By the end of the day, I think I was a much better skier.

Of course, there *was* a lot of flirting too (no touching though, as everyone was bundled up). We talked about last night on some of those long lift rides. I admitted to Scott I liked him and was attracted to him. I wasn't revealing any secrets there, that was pretty obvious. But I was married. Happily married.

Scott said he liked me too, and was hot for me. He promised Mike would never find out.

I was coming to a crossroads. Mike and I both were into our game. How far did we want to go with it?

But I knew one thing. If I *did* take the next step with Scott, I didn't want him to think I was cheating on Mike. I didn't want to be a cheating wife. I mean, there was Joey, but no one but me and Joey knew about that. Anyways, with Scott, I didn't want to feel like a cheating wife. I didn't want him to think I was cheating,

That meant I had to tell Scott about our game. And *that* meant telling Scott about Mike's fantasy of seeing me with other men. I knew that would be a betrayal of Mike unless I had his permission. So we needed to talk.

———◉———

When we got back to the house, Mike wasn't home yet. That kind of surprised me since it was getting dark. I checked around. I found out he went skiing by himself. I sighed. That was so like my husband.

I wasn't worried yet. He was a big boy and we were at Stowe. Not exactly the wilderness. I took a shower and did my hair and makeup. Then I had to decide what to wear. I put on a short skirt and thigh high tights. I wore the thigh highs for Mike, not Scott. I swear—I'm telling the truth. To prove it, I also put on Mia flats with the ribbons that tie up my legs. Mike looooves when I wear those flats.

I guess I was feeling guilty about spending so much time with Scott, and leaving him alone. Also. I was hoping to get Mike in a good mood, so I could talk to him about Scott.

I didn't wear a bra under my green turtleneck. That I did for Scott. He got so turned on last night when he saw me braless in the chemise. I wanted to turn Scott on. I wanted him to want me as much as I wanted him.

When I joined the others, the party was just getting going. Mike still wasn't home. Now I was starting to get worried. I drank water instead of alcohol in case we had to go look for him.

I tried to avoid Scott. I needed to talk to Mike first. But he sought me out. "Nice outfit," he whispered to me as he looked at my braless tits. "I saved us seats at the fire," he said, motioning to one of the sofas next to the big wood fireplace.

"Mike's not home yet," I said, worriedly scanning around the room to see if he got home without me noticing.

"I'm sure he's fine," Scott said. He motioned to the window. "Stowe's got night skiing. Ski patrol's 24/7."

I looked at the window Scott was pointing. He was right. The night skiers were starting to take over the mountain. Mike was probably fine. Stowe has some long, easy runs, like Toll Road, Crossover and Easy Mile. If Mike got on one of those, there's no way he could get in trouble, but it would take a while to get down and then make his way to the house. And if he *did* get in trouble, the ski patrol was everywhere. Scott was right. Mike was fine.

I sat down next to Scott and tried to relax and have fun. I sipped a beer, but nothing stronger, and I declined the joints as they were passed around. I was still worried about Mike even though I knew he was okay.

I got irritated that he went out alone. You've *never* supposed to go skiing alone. But Mike was so shy, no way he would go skiing with people he barely knew. I realized as his wife it was my job to go with him, or at least make sure he paired up with other people. Instead, I went with Scott, and I was so excited to spend the day with him that I didn't take the time to arrange things for Mike. I felt selfish and guilty, and that made me even more worried. Finally, I couldn't stand sitting next to Scott anymore and I pulled Grace and Allie into the kitchen so they could worry with me.

A little while later, Mike finally got home and I practically ran to him. I was so relieved! I hugged and kissed him. When I asked why he was home so late he gave me the brush off and said he wanted to do another run down a black. What the fuck? A black at night? Did he want to break a leg and then die from exposure?

Then I got it. Mike purposely took his time getting home to punish me for spending so much time with Scott. I said, "So this is you punishing me, right?" I said it as a joke, but I was irritated too. I mean, you don't joke about this kind of thing. I was worried sick!

I needed to talk to Mike about Scott but now I was irritated with him. I pulled him into the fireplace room. I sat away from Scott (even though Scott was saving us seats) because I didn't want to give Mike a reason to give me shit.

After a while I realized I was being unfair to Mike. He was my husband after all. *I* was the shit, not him. So I poured him a big glass of his favorite drink, Highland Park scotch. "What, are you trying to get me drunk?" he joked when he saw my big pour.

"I just want you to relax baby," I told him, rubbing his shoulder. Then someone passed a joint to me. I think we both needed to mellow so I shared the joint with Mike. I was hoping once we relaxed I could talk to him about Scott. But then Scott and Mike got into a stupid fight over – of all things – James Bond. I mean, really? Honestly, I thought Mike started it, so that made me irritated with him again.

Eventually we drifted over to where Scott was standing. We socialized with the people there. Mike and I shared another joint. Then all of a sudden he was gone. That's the thing with my husband. I love him to death. But sometimes at parties he just up and disappears.

"So where's hubby?" Scott said to me.

"I don't know," I said irritably.

"If I had a wife who looked as good as you, I'd never let you out of my sight," Scott said. He was looking at my braless chest.

"Just stop, okay," I said with a laugh. I wasn't in the mood for compliments. Although I admit I liked it.

"I want to tell you something," Scott said grabbing my hand.

"What?" I asked.

"Come on," he said pulling my hand.

I shrugged inside and let him lead me out of the fireplace room. We ended downstairs in the game room again.

"Really Scott?" I said looking warily around the room. It was empty again. For some reason, no one but us came in here.

"I just want to talk," he said.

"Okay, then, what?" I asked him. I didn't want to be alone with him. I needed to talk to Mike and I didn't trust myself.

He boldly reached out and cupped my braless breasts. "I'm not the only one noticing you're braless all the time," he said with a grin. "If this is your new style, I approve."

I backed away from him. "You said you wanted to talk," I said, breathing harder. His hands on my breasts had sent bolts of electricity through me, all of them ending up at my clit. I was aching!

"We are talking," Scott said, abruptly pulling me back to him. He was a big man and I was a slim girl, so I was like a rag doll to him. Easy to move around.

He had one hand around my back, holding me there (not that I was pushing away). With his other he fondled and kneaded my breast again. "You do like to show off, don't you Jenny?"

"All girls like attention," I informed him.

"Well, you're getting it," Scott said with a laugh. "You know there's not a guy in here who doesn't want to bend you over a chair and fuck you?"

My cheeks burned from his fondling. And from what he was saying. "People talk about me?" I asked, breathing really hard now.

"Don't play that innocent act with me, Jenny," he said, giving me that lewd, knowing smile again. "We both know you're a cock tease." He pinched my nipple and my lips parted into an O, moaning. Then his lips were on me, kissing me. I kissed him back. It was just like last night. We were making out and fondling each other.

Suddenly Scott pushed me against the pool table, bending me over. He was holding me down with one big hand on my back. With his other he yanked up my skirt, all the way to my waist. He stopped for a moment, looking at my ass and legs. Then he put his foot between mine and kicked my legs apart. Now I was open to him.

———⬦———

I wasn't scared. This was Scotty. All I had to do was say *stop*. At that moment though, with his hand pinning me to the pool table, and his foot forcing my legs apart, I felt helpless and vulnerable. Scott's a big man and I'm small. He's strong. If he wanted to fuck me against my will, I couldn't stop him. At that moment, I fantasized that Scott was about to rape me. It got me so hot I felt dizzy.

Scott yanked my thong down my legs, and I heard him open his zipper. I knew it was getting serious.

"No Scott. I don't want this," I pleaded, my eyes watering up.

"Yes you do!" he growled, moving up behind me, positioning himself. He was right. I *did* want this. And this was exactly how I wanted it. Held down and taken from behind by a powerful, handsome man. It was exactly how I fantasized it.

But I needed to talk to Mike.

"No Scott, stop," I said more forcefully. Scott heard the edge in my voice. He hesitated, then let me go. I stood up and turned around. I pulled up my thong and pushed down my skirt.

We were looking warily at each other. "We're gonna fuck. You know that right?" he told me.

I looked at him, breathing hard. Then I pushed passed him like last night and ran upstairs.

CHAPTER 3

I got to the fireplace room, practically panting. My pussy was on fire. Everyone was there. Bobby was playing techno dance music and the party was rocking.

Then I saw Mike. It looked like he was looking for me. *(Author's note: Jen is right. See the end of Chapter 1.)*

I went to him and grabbed his hand. I led him down the hall.

We went to that nook off the back stairs he found yesterday. It gave us privacy to talk. But I didn't know how to start. I looked at my hands, my feet, trying to find the words but they wouldn't come. Yes, we talked about this, we discussed what-ifs, we talked about boundaries, we even make rules. But how do you tell your husband you desperately want to fuck another man?

---————◦◦————---

Jen had a major cum face on. I could tell she wanted to tell me, but she didn't know how. But it was pretty obvious. So, I said, "You want to fuck Scott." It was a statement, not a question.

When she nodded, I said bitterly "Did you fuck last night?"

"No Mike we didn't," she assured me.

"Then what happened?" I said angrily.

Jen looked scared. She knew I'm usually laid back and even-tempered, but when I get angry I can get ugly really fast. Not physical ugly—I'd never hit or harm Jen—but I can say some really mean and hurtful things. After a moment, she said "We kissed. He touched me. My breasts. He fingered me." After a few moments she added, "He made me cum."

29

I got less angry. At least she was telling me the truth. "What else happened? Did you make him cum?"

"No, nothing else happened," she said immediately. "I wanted to talk to you first."

"But you wanted more?" I asked. She nodded.

"You want to fuck him now," I said. She nodded again.

I looked down, processing this information. My heart was pounding. My fantasy was about to happen. It *had* happened, I'd seen it. Jen had kissed another man. He touched her breasts. He fingered her to orgasm.

My cock was so hard. I wanted this! But I *didn't* want it too. Jen's pussy was still all mine. Since we met, only I had been inside her. As soon as Scott fucked her, everything would be different. I knew he was bigger than me, that was apparent yesterday from the bulge in his Speedos. With that big cock, he'd give her more pleasure than me. I just knew it. He'd ruin her for me.

I was so excited I was shaking. Scott was going to *ruin my wife for me*. That thought ... that word, *ruin* – it was so powerful. It made me shiver and my body shake.

"Are you okay?" Jen asked, taking my hand in hers. She could feel me shake.

I nodded. I wasn't able to speak. That's how excited I was. Have you ever been so excited that you weren't able to form words in your mouth? That's how excited I was.

"There's something else," she said hesitantly. She was still holding my hand. "I don't want Scott to think I'm cheating."

I looked at her, not understanding at first. Then I got it. She wanted to tell Scott about our game. About my fantasies.

"Why?" I asked.

"I don't want Scott to think of me that way," Jen said. "I don't want to lose his respect."

My jaw dropped. "He wants to fuck a married woman, and you're worried about *him* respecting *you*?!" I said incredulously. "And this isn't the first time! He got Allie to cheat on RH!"

"That wasn't cheating. They were broken up," Jen said.

"Why are you always defending him?"

"I'm not defending him. I'm just saying what happened," Jen insisted. "He's really nice Mike. If you'd just give him a chance—."

I winced at the way she was talking about Scott. Her words were like a physical blow, like a punch across my face. She *was* defending him. Going on and on about how great a guy he was. It hurt hearing her. It was like twisting a knife in my gut.

She saw it too, the pain in my face, and said, "Okay, I'm sorry. I know he's a player. I know that. But this is about me. I said it wrong before. It's not about *Scott* losing respect for me. It's about *me* losing respect for me."

What Jen said made me feel better. But she was a marketing chick. She knew how to sell. She always knew what to say. If Message 1 doesn't work, try Message 2.

"I'll be humiliated if you tell Scott about me," I told her. "He'll have something over me."

"No he won't—."

"Yes he will!" I insisted. "I fantasize about my wife with other men. How do you think that'll play out when you tell Scott that? Talk about respect. He'll lose all respect for me. He'll laugh at me. Whenever I see him, he'll hold it over me."

Jen hesitated. Then, she squeezed my hand, and very gently said, "Mike baby ... if he fucks me, isn't that the same thing?"

I stared at Jen. I realized she was right. If Scott was fucking my wife, he would think he had one over on me. At least if he knew Jen had my permission, it would show I had some control over it. I was sharing Jen with him. I was *letting* him fuck her.

But did I want Jen to fuck Scott, of all people? In the perfect world – the way I played it out in my head – Jen would have sex with my best friend Sam. He was single, no girlfriend, and I knew he was hot for her. I wanted something more controlled for our first time. Sam would never try to take Jen from me. He would never demean me, or hold it over my head.

But I'd never told Jen about how Sam was attracted to her. First, because I knew she wasn't attracted to him. Second, because I thought she'd find it too weird since they were friends.

"I don't know Jen," I told her honestly. "I know you want an answer now. But I don't have one for you. You going to have to wait. I need more time."

"Okay," Jen said, looking down at her hands. She was silent for long moments. I couldn't tell what she was thinking, or feeling. Disappointment? Relief? I couldn't tell.

"You really scared me before. Skiing by yourself, and staying out so late, after dark," she finally said. "That was a real shit move."

"I'm sorry," I said. "I was really jealous. I am jealous."

"Then why did we start this?" she said. She wasn't mad. She was just trying to understand.

"I'm trying to figure it out myself," I said, feeling embarrassed. "Feeling jealous ... feeling ignored, like I did yesterday and today ... like you wanted to be with Scott more than me ... for some reason it makes it more intense. I get so excited I start shaking and I can't stop."

"But you get upset too," Jen said.

"Yeah ..." I admitted. We were silent for long moments. Then I admitted, "I saw you last night. With Scott."

"When?"

"In the game room. I saw you together," I said.

Jen's eyes went wide. "And you let it happen?"

Her answer surprised me. Because at the time it didn't feel like I had any say in the matter. But she was right. I could've stopped it. I could have walked in and punched Scott in the face. But I let it happen.

"Yeah, I let it happen," I said. Then I admitted, "It was the most exciting thing I've ever seen."

Jen stared at me. I said, "I'm not saying I won't agree to it. I'm just saying I'm not agreeing to it now. I can't. This is a big step. I'm not ready. I need to think about it."

"Okay," Jen said. We hugged and kissed. We made love. We fell asleep in that nook, spooning each other.

The next day we went skiing on our own. I proved to Jen I wasn't bullshitting when I said I went down some blacks. It was a really good morning. Really good. At noon, we said our goodbyes and drove home.

CHAPTER 4

A few days later, I gave Jen permission. I thought about it non-stop. What decided it for me was what I said before. This was the only time in our lives we'd be able to experiment. Soon we would start a family. We both agreed our game would stop the moment she got pregnant. Jen was already 29, and we wanted 2 or even 3 kids. I didn't want her pregnant at 35; it wasn't safe. We had a year to play, maybe less.

So I decided to go for it. Jen would have a wild fling. With Scott, then after that ended, maybe someone else. We would get this craziness out of our system. Then we'd go back to being a boring monogamous married couple again. But we'd have exciting memories forever.

We decided on Friday night. I picked Friday because then we would have the entire weekend to reconnect. Also, I made Jen promise to be home by 1am. She planned to come home first after work, to change, so that would give them only about 5 hours. I was more worried about them spending time alone, than the sex. I already could tell Jen had a crush on Scott and I didn't want it to develop into something more.

Once she was home from work, I watched Jen get dressed. She didn't mind. In fact, she seemed to enjoy all the attention I was giving her.

Jen wore a sexy black dress that ended above her knees and hugged her body. She wore a thong and thigh high stockings underneath, but no bra. Scott seemed to like when she went braless.

Jen finished the outfit with 4-inch high heels.

"Those are some high heels," I said, looking at her feet.

"I know. Can you believe I'm wearing high heels?" Jen said with a laugh. "And these are really high. Four inches."

"I can't believe you can walk in them," I said.

"What really makes it hard is the stiletto heels," Jen said. "I'm getting used to them though. Aren't they pretty? They're Christian Louboutin. All his shoes had red bottoms. See?"

Jen turned slightly so I could see the red bottoms of the heels.

"They look expensive," I said.

"You said I could buy new clothes," Jen said cautiously. She knew I was frugal, especially since we were trying to save to buy our first house.

"It's okay," I hurriedly assured her. "Your legs look amazing in those heels."

Jen smiled, looking relieved. "Guys look at me more, since I've started wearing really high heels," she said. "That's what you want, right? That's our game."

"Yeah," I agreed.

"I bought some others, for work, and when we go out. So you'll see when we get the credit card bill. I got a couple pairs of Jimmy Choos. But I like Christian Louboutin's the most because I think the red soles are really cute. These are called *So Kates*. He named them after Kate Moss. And Kate Middleton wears them."

I nodded slowly. Shoes had names? And I knew who Kate Moss and Kate Middleton were of course. But Christian Louboutin and Jimmy Choo? I'd never heard of them before.

I noticed a little plastic bag next to her purse. I looked inside. It was a box of condoms.

I took it out and studied the box. The box said "Extra Thin – Feels Natural" and "XXL." I turned the box over in my hand. Jen had actually gone to a drug store and bought condoms. For her date tonight.

I felt stunned. This was real. It was going to happen.

"Just in case. You know?" Jen said, seeing me holding the box.

"Oh, yeah," I sputtered out, not knowing what else to say.

"I went back on the pill," she said. "Obviously."

"Yeah ... obviously."

"But, you know, the pill's not 100%. And we don't know where Scott's been."

"Yeah, absolutely, makes sense," I sputtered out.

I was beginning to feel like an idiot with my mindless responses. I hadn't even thought about birth control. And now the reality of what we were doing was really hitting me. Another man's penis was going to be inside my wife. Scott was going to be inside her. He was going to kiss her, and touch her everywhere, and then he was going to penetrate her with his cock.

He might be in her mouth too. Who was I kidding. Of course his cock was going to be in her mouth. And then he was going to cum. Inside her. And without protection, his sperm might impregnate her. Impregnate my wife. My Jen.

I stared at the condom box. "Extra Thin – Feels Natural." What if the condom breaks while he's inside her? Or falls off when he pulls out? "Are you ovulating?" I asked, feeling panicked.

"No. This is the safest time of the month for me. But I'll make Scotty wear a condom. I promise," Jen assured me.

I nodded my head. I hated when she called him Scotty. I hated it.

"Have you told him?" I asked. I meant about our game. About my fantasies.

"I'm telling him tonight," Jen said. "Are you okay?" she asked, putting her hand on my knee. I was shaking again.

"Yeah. This is just really exciting," I said with a weak smile.

Her iPhone buzzed. She looked at it. "It's Scott. He's downstairs."

I nodded. I was happy he didn't come to the door. I didn't want to see him. Jen gave me a smile and kiss. Then she was gone.

———◉———

"So I need to tell you something," I told Scott when we were at his apartment. I was drinking a Cosmo and he was drinking Jack and Coke. "I'm not cheating on Mike. He knows what's happening. I have his permission."

Scott's eyes opened wide and he sat back on the sofa, stunned. Then he got it. "It turns him on. You fucking guys."

"We've never done this before," I said. "This is the first time."

"But I'm right," he pressed.

I hesitated, then said "Yes, you're right."

"Huh ...," he said, shaking his head as he processed this information. He didn't look surprised. "You know it makes sense. You were with me most of the time at Stove and he didn't complain."

"He was pissed, Scott," I told him.

"But he didn't do anything," Scott said. "Most guys would've punch me, or hauled your ass out of there. But Mike just let it happen. Now I get it. He was watching me with you. Getting off on it. His dick was probably hard the entire time."

I shrugged. Scott was probably right. In fact, I knew he was right, because whenever I touched Mike at Stowe he had an erection.

"So why didn't we hook up last weekend? Why'd you make me wait?"

"I told you, this is our first time," I said.

Scott nodded slowly, as he processed this new information about me and Mike. "He needed to figure out if he really wanted to do this," he said.

"We both did," I said. I was impressed Scott was catching up so fast. But then, it wasn't really complicated.

"So I'm your first. I'm really flattered Jenny. I'm not kidding, I really am," Scott said. I smiled. I could tell he was sincere, not just bullshitting me.

"I don't want a one-night stand, a hook up with a stranger I meet in a bar," I explained. "I want it to be a friend. Someone I'm attracted to, but a friend."

"Well, now I'm even more flattered," Scott said, smiling at me. I smiled back. We stayed like that for a few moments, just smiling at each other. Then he moved closer until we were almost touching. "I think we've waited long enough," he said.

"I think so too," I said. Then we were kissing.

⸺⸺●⸺⸺

Our sex was fireworks. I can't remember it all. That's how intense it was. All I know is, it was the *best sex* of my life. And I came really hard. More than once. On top of that, Scott said it was just as good for him.

Scott didn't want to wear a condom. He promised he was clean and I believed him. I told Scott if it was just me, I wouldn't make him wear a condom. But I had Mike to think about. I insisted and Scott put one on. That's what I mean about Scott. He's a really nice person. I think if Mike made an effort to know him, they could be friends.

I'd seen Scott without a shirt, but this was the first time I saw him completely nude. Wow. I kinda knew what to expect from Allie, but wow. His body is so incredibly amazing. And it's not all from lifting, he's really athletic. He wrestled in college – and that kind of threw me for a loop when he told me that, because of Joey who wrestled in high school. Scotty's in a basketball league right now. He says it's one step below semi-pro and really competitive. He wants me to go to one of his games. I said I would, it sounds like fun.

Scotty has the most amazing cock. It's long. It's longer than my forearm, so long I had to measure it. Eleven inches. *Eleven freaking inches.* I've seen bigger in internet porn but not in real life. He's not as thick as Joey, but he's way thick enough. Like Joey's, I can't get my hand around Scott's shaft. He really stretched me, and I love that sensation.

Lengthwise, Scotty has a few inches on Joey. I think I now know what it means for a boy to bottom out in a girl. I experienced it for the first time with Scott. It was the most amazing feeling when I felt the head of his penis press against my cervix. It was a weird feeling too. Not weird-bad, just weird-different. But I liked it. It was amazing knowing that Scotty was literally giving me all I could take.

Scotty doesn't have just a great body, he knows how to use it too. I kinda expected that, from what Allie told me. And also, from the way he carries himself. Like, he's good in bed and he knows it. Yeah, he's kinda full of himself that way, but he can back it up, because he *is* an amazing lover. He learned my body, all my erogenous zones, in like, 10 seconds. He's a freaking awesome kisser! He spent a lot of time kissing and touching me – everywhere – before trying to get inside me. When he finally got between my legs, I was practically begging for it!

The first time I came was with Scotty inside me. I was breathing hard and sweating – we both were – because it was taking a lot of time and effort for Scotty to get inside me. I guess I was tighter than he was used to. There came a point I felt so full – almost *too full*—and then I looked between my legs, and he still had inches to go! That's when I came.

It was kinda like with Joey, but different. Joey's thicker, but at some point, if I'm stretched so tight, any extra girth doesn't really make any difference. I *did* notice Scott's extra length though. He reached places in me no man had ever touched before.

The second time was after our first intercourse. After we recovered and joked around a little, Scotty went to work on me again. He got between my legs and started eating me out. That surprised me, because in my experience, really hot players like Scott don't do oral, at least not all the way. But Scotty didn't stop licking and sucking me until I came! He was good too. Not as good as Mike. But he was good, and different, and new, so I had a really intense orgasm.

The third time I came was our second intercourse. The first time he was gentle, I guess to let us get used to each other. It was missionary that time, and he fondled and kissed me the whole time. It was more like making love than fucking.

The second time, though, was *definitely* fucking. It was harder and rougher. It was more for his pleasure than mine, and I guess he felt justified because he had just got me off with his tongue. Scotty flipped me over onto my hands and knees and took me from behind. He fucked me really hard – *really hard* – and I loved it! I came hard on his cock. It was the most intense of my three orgasms (and the other two were really awesome too). Scotty came so hard I was afraid he was going to blow the condom off. But when he pulled out it was still on.

It was pass midnight and I needed to go to be home by 1am. Scotty said he had a great time. I told him I did too. He said it was the best sex he had in a long time. I told him it might be the best sex of my life! Then he admitted it was probably the best sex of his life too, but he didn't want to say it unless I said it first. I laughed and punched his arm, and called him a jerk.

He asked if we could do it again. I told him I had to ask Mike. I told Scott not to make fun of Mike about his fantasies. Especially since they were the reason I was here with him. He promised he wouldn't.

He asked if I was going to make him wear a condom the next time. I reminded him that I wasn't sure if there was even going to be a next time, as I had to talk to Mike. And anyways, I trusted him but I had a responsibility to my husband, so yes, he had to use a condom unless we both got tested. He said he trusted me, but I said I'd never ask him to get tested unless I got tested too. Then Scotty hugged and kissed me, and said he just wanted to be inside me skin-to-skin. It was an incredibly sweet thing to say, and it made my heart melt. I told him I wanted that too, but first I had to talk to Mike.

While we were lazing around after our first intercourse, I touched his arms. "These are so awesome," I gushed, tracing my fingertips along the images of his tattoo sleeves.

"You're into tats?" Scott asked.

"Yeah," I said, mesmerized by the beautiful tattoo art.

"You got this one," Scott said, touching my hip. I had a small black tattoo there. It was on my hip bone below my waistline so you couldn't see it when I was dressed, but it was visible when I wore a bikini (depending on the bikini).

"Yeah," I said. "It's the Japanese character for love. Mike hates it."

"Why?"

"Well, first he hates tats. But mostly the way I got it. I was a senior in high school. Both Colin and I got into Penn State. He was my boyfriend then. I thought I loved him. I thought we were going to get married eventually. He wanted me to get tatted with his name."

"Seriously?"

"I mean, I'm not stupid, I wasn't going to do it," I said. "But Colin wanted something, and I wanted a tat too, so I got this. I told him it was a symbol of our love."

"And he believed it?" Scott said with a laugh.

"Well, it was true back then," I told him honestly. "But you see why Mike hates it? I got inked for Colin. And see how it looks? The right side almost looks like a C. That's what Mike thinks. I told him he's crazy but ...."

"But doesn't that push his cuckold buttons?" Scott said.

"Don't be an ass Scott," I said frowning at him.

"That's just the word for it," he said, holding his hands out in surrender. "But you see my point?"

Actually, I did see his point. And it made me wonder .... But I didn't want to talk to Scott about it. "Anyways, I really like your tat sleeves," I said, again running my fingertips along the intricate art.

"You gonna get another one?" Scott asked.

"I'd like to."

"Where?"

"Um, I don't know," I said. "Nothing like your sleeves. Maybe a bracelet around my ankle or arm. A little flower or tribal on the back of my neck. Or some writing on my wrist. I don't know."

"You've thought a lot about it," Scott said. "What would you write?"

"I don't know," I said with a shrug. "Maybe my babies' names. Anyways, it's not going to happen. Mike's vetoed it."

"So do it anyway."

"He's my husband Scott."

"And you've having sex with another man," Scott pointed out. "You don't think that changes things?"

CHAPTER 5

The waiting was agony. I experienced major cuckold angst, the kind you read in stories. I masturbated twice, and could've beaten off more, but the depression I felt each time after cumming was so intense I had to stop.

I watched the clock constantly. Minutes seemed like hours. I looked at our wedding pictures and watched videos of our last vacation together. Anything to feel connected to her.

I wondered what she was doing with Scott. But I had to stop thinking about it. It made me intensely jealous and also incredibly hot. It made me want to masturbate again but I couldn't face the depression that I knew would come after.

Finally, I heard a key in the door. I think I stopped breathing as the door swung open. And then she was there.

Jen looked tired. Her hair and clothes were disheveled. She held her high heels in her left hand. She looked happy and satisfied. She had a glow about her. I realized she looked freshly fucked.

That's when it really hit me. Jen was now a hot wife. She'd been with another man. She kissed him. Let him touch her naked body. Let him inside her. Let him make her cum. Everything was different now. Everything. I was no longer her only lover. Probably I wasn't even her best lover anymore. Maybe eventually she might not turn to me at all to take care of her sexual needs.

As these dark thoughts flashed through my head, I was incredibly jealous and experienced major cuckold angst. I was hot too, my cock rock hard. Most of all though, I loved Jen. I loved her now more than ever.

It was late, past 1am, and we were both tired. But we were too wired to sleep. I didn't reclaim my wife immediately. I pampered her. I drew a bath and rubbed her shoulders and neck while she relaxed in the hot water with her eyes closed. I shampooed her hair, using my fingers to massage her scalp and rub her temples.

I used to do this when we first started dating. Back then, I couldn't believe Jenny Paige Johnson, the most beautiful and popular girl at Penn State, actually wanted to date me. I couldn't believe it when she said she loved me. I couldn't believe it when she agreed to marry me. I couldn't believe it when she said her marriage vows, promising herself only to me. So all during that time I did more than love Jen. I worshipped her. I did things like I was doing now, pampering her in the bath tub.

Somewhere along the way I lost that. I lost my obsession with Jen. Maybe because I started getting successful at work, and I was drawing the attention of other pretty girls (like Elaine). But now I was obsessed again. It's ironic it took other men desiring my wife to make me worship her again. But that's exactly what happened. Now, the only thing I was able to think about was Jen.

We got into bed, laying on our sides and looking at each other. Up to then we hadn't even mentioned Scott. I said, "You did it?"

"Yes," she said.

"How was it?"

"You want me to tell the truth, right?"

When I nodded, she gushed "It was incredible!"

I was silent for a moment, processing that. "Are you alright Mike?" she asked.

I hesitated, then said "I'm just trying to get used to the idea. You've been with another man. We've taken a big step."

"Yes," she agreed.

"Is he big?" I asked. I desperately wanted to know this. But I didn't too.

Jen nodded. "I measured him," she said. "He's a little more than 11 inches. And like this." She formed a circle with her hand, with her thumb and middle finger separated by almost two inches.

"Wow, that's big," I said impressed. My heart was pounding in my chest. "You measured him?"

"We were joking around," she said.

I nodded, silent for a moment. Jen had never measured me. Never asked or tried to measure me. Maybe it wasn't worth it. I knew I was small. I looked it up. The average penis (erect) is about 5 inches long and 4 and a half inches around. I was smaller than average. So that meant Scott was more than twice as big as me.

"How did you get that inside you?" I wondered.

"It wasn't easy," Jen said with a laugh, as if she was remembering the effort. "It was easier the second time."

"So you did it more than once?"

"Twice," she said with a nod of her pretty head.

"Intercourse I mean," I said. "You had intercourse twice."

"... I mean, yeah baby," Jen said hesitantly. "That's what you wanted right?"

"Yeah, I'm just trying to picture that big cock inside you," I said with a helpless laugh. My cock was rock hard and I was beyond excited. So excited my body was shaking again.

"Calm down baby," Jen said soothingly, rubbing my arm.

"I can't," I said with another helpless laugh. "You came with him inside you."

"Yes."

"Both times?"

"Yes Mike."

"His cock made you cum?" I asked urgently. "You weren't touching yourself. His cock made you cum."

"Yes baby," she said softly, soothingly rubbing my arm again.

"He came fucking you?" I asked.

"Yes but I made him wear a condom," she said.

"Did he cum a lot?"

Jen thought about it. "Honestly, I don't know. He used tissues to take the condom off so I didn't see."

I was silent, processing this information. I had more questions, a lot more, but my head was spinning from excitement. I couldn't think straight. "So you came twice?" I finally asked.

"Three times actually," she said. When I looked questioning at her, she said, "He went down on me once."

"Oh," I said, surprised. For some reason I'd assumed going down on her was going to be reserved for me. But we'd never talked about it so it wasn't her fault. It bothered me though. It meant nothing was reserved exclusively for me.

Jen saw I was upset but misread the reason. She smiled encouragingly at me and said, "Scotty's not as good as you. You're the best."

I smiled back at her. I welcomed the compliment, and I could tell she was telling the truth. But still I felt the angst of knowing my wife's body was no longer exclusively mine. And it bothered me whenever she called him "Scotty."

Jen's eyelids were getting heavy. I could tell she was close to falling asleep. We had the whole weekend to talk about this. So finally it was time to reclaim my wife. I got on top of her and Jen opened her legs, welcoming me into her. Our sex was short though. I was so turned on I lasted only a few strokes. Jen didn't seem to mind though. No doubt she'd gotten enough from Scott.

⟹⟩◉⟨⟸

I was afraid the next morning would be awkward between us, having to face the reality of what happened in the clear-headedness of the new day. But it wasn't awkward at all. Mostly because Jen lavished attention on me, just like I did to her last night.

We showered together. We hadn't done that in a long time. I washed her hair and rubbed her neck and shoulders, like last night, the way I used to. Jen really responded to all the attention I was giving her. It was like, the more attention I gave her, the more she gave me. I felt like what people said was true, sharing your wife with another man actually brought you closer together.

We had lunch and shared a bottle of wine, and got tipsy. That was another thing we hadn't done in a long time, getting drunk with the sun high in the sky. We went into a jewelry store and I bought Jen a simple gold chain. I whispered into her ear, "You wear it around your ankle. It means you're a hot wife."

Jen giggled and let me attach it around her left ankle. The older salesman didn't say anything, but he smiled like he knew what was going on.

At home we fucked again. It was the 2nd time that day (we also had sex in the shower). It was like we were newlyweds again. It was amazing. We were closer than ever, and I was incredibly happy. I think Jen was just as happy too.

The entire weekend we didn't talk about Scott. We finally did in bed Sunday night, as we lay on our sides and looked at each other. "Scotty asked if we could do it again," Jen cautiously said.

I slowly nodded. It wasn't a surprise. "Do you want to?" I asked.

"...yes," she hesitantly answered. Then she quickly added, "If you want me to."

I smiled indulgently. "Always the truth, and never sugar coat it," I said, reminding her of one of our rules.

She smiled. "Okay then, yes, I'd like to do it again."

"Something about Scott. I don't like him. But I'm glad you're doing it with someone you like," I said.

Jen looked relieved when I said that. "Thanks for understanding. I don't want it to be one night stands, or a guy at a swingers club. It's better for me with a friend."

"It's better for me too," I admitted. "It makes me jealous knowing you're with someone you like. But it gets me hot too."

"Okay," Jen said. I could see she was processing what I said, trying to understand it.

"But remember, I'm traveling this week. I don't want anything to happen while I'm away," I told her.

"Of course not baby. I would never do something behind your back," Jen promised.

CHAPTER 6

Tuesday night, Joey called and invited me to go to a party with him tomorrow. He said he was rushing a fraternity and they were having a social where dates were not only welcome but mandatory (the brothers wanted to make sure you weren't a loser before they invited you to join their frat). Joey said he'd have a better chance of pledging if he had a girl with him. He didn't want to ask a girl from school because, in his words, they were "too clingy."

I agreed to go. But I made it clear there wasn't going to be any funny business. I was determined to stop cheating on Mike.

Also, honestly, I was over Joey. After my incredible experience with Scott, I saw Joey for what he was ... a young boy. Blessed with a great body, but still just a boy.

And Scott wasn't cheating, since Mike knew about it, and encouraged it. So I didn't feel like I was doing a bad thing when I was with Scott, the way I felt with Joey.

After work the next day I went into the bathroom to change. I needed to morph from chic advertising chick to bubbly college coed. Off went my Fendi designer dress, Agent Provocateur stockings and Jimmy Choo high heels.

All these clothes were new. And I had more new clothes, lingerie and high heels in my closet at home. I was spending a lot of money lately, but I had to dress to impress to attract male attention. That was the whole point of our game. And I especially wanted to keep Scott interested in me.

I knew my spending was cutting into our downpayment savings and delaying our dream of buying our first home, but Mike seemed okay with it. He really liked the way I was dressing sexy every day for work. He liked watching me get dressed in the morning, and get undressed at night. And I loved all the attention he was giving me.

I stuffed my clothes into my bag and squeezed into skinny jeans and an off-the-shoulder long sleeve top. It was the same top I'd worn before. I also wore my black Converse high tops. I washed off all my makeup and brushed on just a little Urban Decay brownish-red lipstick, and wore my hair down.

Looking into the mirror, I hoped I looked like a college student (since I was wearing my hair longer nowadays, I think that helped). Joey and I had already agreed on a story. I was his grad student friend visiting from Penn State. Just as I was about to leave, I remembered to take off my wedding and engagement rings. I stuffed them into my purse. There were slight indents on my ring finger, where the rings had been a moment ago, but there was nothing I could do about that.

Scott was waiting for me when I opened the bathroom door. I frowned because I felt like he was stalking me. I'd been avoiding him since the weekend. I wanted to keep him interested in me, but I was married after all, and I didn't want rumors flying around work. Also, while I knew Mike was as into our game as me, he was also conflicted about it, so I felt the best thing to do was to take it slow with Scott.

Still, though, my heart did a flip because Scott *was* stalking me.

"Scott I'm late," I said moving past him.

"We need to talk about the weekend," Scott said grabbing my wrist. I looked around nervously. We were in the freaking hallway outside our offices!

"Will you be quiet!" I hissed in a whispered voice. "Mike is traveling. We haven't been able to talk."

"Let's get together Saturday," Scott whispered. "At your place. Mike can watch. That's probably what he wants."

"What, you're an expert now?" I sarcastically whispered back.

"He's not that hard to figure out," Scott said with a shrug.

I thought about it for a moment. Then I whispered, "I'll ask him. But if he says yes it'll be Friday."

"Why?"

"Because he likes the whole weekend to reconnect with me," I told Scott.

Scott chuckled, grinning knowingly at me. "To reclaim you, right?" he said.

I didn't say anything, but I couldn't help grinning back. Scotty *was* figuring out Mike.

Scott looked me up and down. He said, "You look good. You've got that sexy / cute thing going on. You look like a fucking teenager."

I couldn't help laughing. Then, feeling wicked, I gave him a mischievous grin and whispered "Scotty, are you into barely legal girls?"

He grinned back and whispered, "I've had my share."

We both laughed. Then I tugged down my top a little so it fell off my shoulder. As he looked at my bare skin, I whispered, "Oops. I guess I forgot to put on a bra."

Scott shook his head as he said, "God, Jenny, you kill me."

I looked down and saw he had an erection in his pants. Mission accomplished! Then I moved passed him, feeling triumphant and giddy.

The fraternity party was fun! I was nervous at first, afraid the kids would see through my disguise and figure out I was an almost 30-year-old married woman. But no one did. Everyone accepted my story of being a grad student from Penn State.

Once I was passed that anxiety, I found myself having fun. Not only did I look like a college student, I felt like I was in college again. It was so much fun!

On top of that, I didn't have to lie to Mike. I told him I was hanging with Joey at a college party and he encouraged me to go. Not as part of the game of course. Mike always worried about Joey, and he was all for me checking on him. He didn't know his younger friend was a pussy hound!

Joey held my hand, or had his arm around me the entire party. I couldn't exactly stop him as we were supposed to be on a date. When he touched me though – like when he tried to squeeze my ass – or tried to kiss me, I wiggled away. More than once I had to whisper into his ear, "No funny business, remember?"

Even when Joey wasn't trying to grope me, he was looking at me. Especially my mouth. And my ass. And my tits. Especially my tits. Since I was braless, my nipples dented the soft fabric of my top. Joey wasn't the only boy to notice. I was very popular at the party, and I loved it. It was like being in college again, when I always got so much attention. It really fed my ego and made me feel good about myself.

Joey gave me a tour of the fraternity house. He led me upstairs and showed me the bedroom he'd get if they accepted him into the frat. It was empty now because the brother who had it last was doing an internship for a congressman in DC.

I was kinda tipsy on beer, so when Joey pulled me into his arms and kissed me, I didn't stop him immediately. In fact, I kissed him back for a few moments. Then I pushed away and said, "Come on Joey. We can't do this."

"Come on Jen, I know you want this," Joey said confidently, and before I knew it, he had his pants down and his cock out. He was rock hard, his thick cock curving in towards his stomach.

"God Joey, put it away," I said chastising, but I didn't look away. I found myself comparing Joey to Scott. Joey was thicker, but Scott was almost as thick. And Scott was noticeably longer. It made me remember how stretched and full I felt with Scott inside me. I got hot thinking about Scott, and here I was standing in front of Joey, with his smaller yet still very impressive manhood out there for the world to see. I found my resolve to end things with Joey dissolving away.

"Fuck it," I said, pulling off my top as I walked the few steps to Joey. Maybe this was why I'd gone braless. A part of me knew – or hoped? – it would end this way.

Suddenly I was on Joey's lap, naked from the waist up, my arms around his neck, sucking face with him.

Joey hurriedly unbuttoned my skinny jeans as I kicked off the Converse high tops. He struggled to peel my skinny jeans off, and I helped him by wiggling my button. Joey kicked off his jeans and then he was on top of me. In a flash, Joey had my ankles on his shoulders and he was balls deep inside me, ramming me with his thick cock.

I knew he wasn't wearing a condom. I was on the pill now, but I had to think about Mike. I knew Joey was sexually active. He was a player. He no doubt got a lot of girls into his bed. I had to think about Mike.

"Joey, condom," I said. He frowned at me, but then got a condom from his wallet. He rolled the condom down his long thick shaft. Then he pushed into me. He started fucking me.

We were both panting and sweating when I guess some people heard us, because a few of Joey's future frat brothers walked into the room. I was mortified at being seen, but at the same time there wasn't anything I could do about it. I mean, I was under Joey, impaled on his cock, my legs on his shoulders, and he was way bigger than me. I was completely under his control, and if he wanted to let his frat brothers watch him fuck me, then I was helpless to do anything about it.

The prospect was so humiliating. My body trembled. I looked into Joey's face, wondering what he was going to do. At that moment, one of the guys touched my foot that was hanging off Joey's shoulder. He was young with red hair and freckles covered his face. He looked into my eyes as he pulled off my sock. He continued looking into my eyes as he pulled the sock off my other foot. My cheeks went red as this young boy removed the last stitch of clothing on my body. I had never felt so humiliated!

There were more boys now in the room. They crowded around us, all of them looking at me. Joey wasn't pressed against me so the boys had a clear view of my naked body. They could also see Joey's big cock pounding my pussy.

Then the red-headed boy began rubbing the bottom of my foot with his thumb. It was too much. I groaned as this boy who looked younger than Joey touched me. I felt like I was about to cum. I thought how even more humiliating that would be, if these young college boys watched as I came. My body trembled even more, and I was on the brink of cumming.

Another boy took hold of my other bare foot. And it seemed they were all closer now, looking into my face.

"Joey ...," I said desperately as my cheeks burned with helpless humiliation.

Then Joey looked to the side and over his shoulder. He noticed his future frat brothers for the first time. He screamed "Get the fuck out!"

The frat brothers filed out of the bedroom. But they took their time, taking lingering looks at my face and naked body. I hoped to god no one had videoed me with their phone.

I was so close. As soon as the door closed, I let myself go. My back arched and I cried out as my orgasm hit.

Joey came soon after, and he shot his load into me.

"What the fuck Joey?" I said between pants.

"I didn't see them," Joey said. He was breathing hard too. "I swear."

I decided to believe him. I mean, what else could I do? It wasn't like I could complain to Mike.

I hurriedly dressed and left the frat party. I wasn't mad at Joey, but I didn't want to face his future frat brothers. I leaned against the door of the yellow checked car as I taxied home. My head was still trying to process what had just happened. But I couldn't help smiling, and my smile turned into a giggle. *I felt so alive!* I was wicked and sinful, and I loved it.

Did I feel guilty for cheating on my husband again? Yes I did.

But probably not as much as I should have. Maybe because of our game. I mean, Mike wanted me to fuck other men. I was sure he never thought it would be with his 18-year-old friend Joey. But still, I think our game helped lessen the guilt I felt over being unfaithful again.

CHAPTER 7

I lavished attention on Mike when he got home. I wanted to make up for Joey. Also though, I was happy, so I wanted him to be happy.

After we had sex, we were lying in bed. My head was on his chest and his arm was around me. "Can I ask you something?" I asked, gently stroking his chest. When he nodded, I said, "You know my tat? Is it part of your fantasy?"

I felt Mike's body stiffen and I knew I was onto something (Scott had guessed it the other day). "What do you mean?" he said. He was playing dumb but I could tell there was something there.

Of course I wasn't going to say Scott figured it out, so I said "I was thinking about the game, and all that's happened. After we got serious and I told you how I got the tat, you got so mad. You screamed "Colin branded you!" You were so mad I thought you were going to hit me."

"I'd never hit you Jen," he said immediately.

"I know baby," I told him, rubbing his arm. "But I didn't know you as well then. You were so mad. But then you were all over me. I don't think we left the apartment all weekend, we fucked so much."

We smiled at each other, both of us remembering. "Anyways, I'm wondering if my tat is part of your fantasy."

Mike didn't say anything for a long time. Finally, in a low voice, he said "I think about it a lot. Whenever I see it, it reminds me he put his mark on you. It looks like a C." He was referring to the right side of the Japanese "love" symbol.

"It doesn't," I insisted. "If anything it looks like an L."

"But I think of it as Colin's mark," Mike said.

Mike was hard again. I took his cock in my hand and slowly stroked him. "So it's part of your fantasy?" I asked again. I wanted to know. How deep did his kinky fantasies go?

"It didn't start that way. But it evolved to that," Mike said. He shrugged and said, "I don't understand it myself."

I gave him an understanding smile and said, "Fantasies are like that baby. They just happen. There's no understanding about it."

Mike smiled back at me, and I could tell he appreciated my understanding. I decided to tell him my deepest, darkest fantasy. I said, "I have a crazy fantasy too."

"What?" he said, suddenly interested.

"I have a rape fantasy," I told him. I quickly added "A lot of girls have it. It's all over the internet. And I don't want to get raped. No girl does. It's more like, I want to be controlled. I want to feel helpless."

"Like a sub?" Mike asked.

"Yeah, but not like 50 Shades. I don't wanna be tied down or whipped. I wanna be helpless. Controlled. Used. Humiliation's a big part of it."

I could tell he didn't understand, so I said "Colin used to make fun of my breasts. He used to say he was going to buy me real tits when he got his first NFL contract, and he'd say that in front of everyone. Freshman year at Penn State, we went to Daytona Beach for spring break. He made me join a wet t-shirt contest. I had to take my bikini top off under my t-shirt. Then they soaked us with water. All the other girls had big boobs."

"It was the most humiliating experience of my life standing on that stage. I felt like everyone was laughing at me. Then when I got back to our group, Colin wouldn't give me back my top. He was drunk. He kept saying "See Jenny's tiny tits? That's why I have to pump them up." I was so humiliated I was crying. Allie railed against him and finally he gave me my top back. I was crying so hard Allie and my other girlfriends didn't talk to Colin the rest of the trip. But you know what? I'd never been so turned on. I fucked Colin so hard the rest of the weekend. I couldn't get enough. Even now, when I masturbate, sometimes I think about that wet t-shirt contest."

Mike stared at me. Like me, he was breathing hard. Finally, he said, "I guess I can see why that's hot."

It was the best thing in the world he could have said! It wasn't judgmental. It wasn't doubt or confusion. It wasn't scorn. Instead, it was love and complete understanding and acceptance. *That* was why I loved and married Mr. Mike Andrews.

"But I can't give you that," he said. "I can't be cruel to you like that."

"I know baby," I said rubbing his chest. "That's why I love you. That's why I married you and not Colin."

Talking about this had gotten me worked up. Mike could tell and he reached down and slowly stroked my pussy. He was hard and I was still stroking him. "Mike baby?" I said. "Scotty wants to see me again. And I want to see him too."

Mike was silent for long moments. Then he said, "I'm afraid you're going to fall in love with him. He's everything I'm not."

"Mike baby, that's exactly why I'll never fall in love with him," I said. "We're friends. I like him. But I'll never feel anything more for Scott. I just want to explore this. When I was with Colin, I didn't understand why I reacted the way I did. Now I do. I want to experience it. Like how you're living out your fantasies. I want to live out mine too. But they go together – our fantasies. You see? We can do this together. It's our game."

Mike slowly nodded, processing this. His cock was still in my hand and he was harder than he'd ever been before. I knew he would agree.

CHAPTER 8

Jen decided to take Friday off. She wanted to buy a new outfit and make dinner for Scott. For me too, but it was Scott who made it a special occasion. Normally I cooked because she liked to work out after work. She was giddy that morning as I was getting ready for work, and it surprised me she didn't even try to hide her excitement from me. But I think it was because we were closer now than ever, and she felt she could share anything with me.

I found out later they talked at least a half dozen times during the day. More laughing and easy banter, a lot of excited talking about their date tonight, but also talking about their shared interests of music, travel, the outdoors, and theater. Scott liked to gamble so he taught Jen the rules of craps. She liked modern art so she talked to him about her favorite artists.

These were the discussions that got me most concerned. They were making a real connection, developing a real relationship. They were already good friends, "best buds" in Jen's words, and now there was the sex. Jen said she would never feel anything more than *like* for Scott, and it was one of our rules to stop the game if she felt herself falling in love. Still I worried. I admit though, the angst and jealousy, and the fear of losing Jen, those things kept me hard all the time. My excitement was so great sometimes I'd start shaking uncontrollably. I'd never experienced such an intense thrill.

As I was about to leave for home, Jen called. She spoke in hushed tones, even though she was alone at home and I was alone in my office. "Mike baby, can you pick up condoms?" she asked in a whispered voice.

"You don't have any?" he said, remember the box of condoms he'd seen.

"Maybe not enough," she said.

Suddenly I was breathing hard. Jen intended to have Scott inside her more than once tonight. "Okay," I said, my voice hoarse with excitement.

"Mike, get the kind that feels natural. I think it's called bareskin, or ultra thin. Something like that," she told me. "And, um, get the biggest size. XXXLs. I got XXLs before, and there's one left, but they're kind of tight on him. I don't want the condom to rip."

"Okay. I'll get XXXLs," I said again. My head was spinning. This was crazy. I was going to buy condoms so my wife could have sex with another man.

Then I realized that Jen was being so careful, and that made me feel better. Also, that was something still reserved solely for me. Jen and I had sex skin-to-skin, but Scott had to wear a condom. That was something.

It was a big something too. Bare sex was way more intimate, not just the skin-to-skin part, but also the sharing of fluids. When you shared fluids, you naturally connected more physically and emotionally. At that moment, I decided Jen would always use condoms with Scott and any other lover she might have in our game. It would be one of our rules.

When I got home, I heard voices inside, and it wasn't just Jen. I frowned when I opened the door and saw Scott. What the fuck? He wasn't supposed to be here for another hour. I was hoping for some alone time with Jen before their "date" started but now that possibility was gone.

Jen was sitting on the sofa with Scott. He had his arm around her, and she was leaning into him with the easy comfort of a girlfriend with her boyfriend. When she saw me though, Jen immediately got up and kissed me. "Hi baby," she said hugging me.

I shook Scott's hand. It was awkward, but what else could I do?

I got a private moment with Jen in the kitchen, and whispered, "Why's he here so early?"

"We were talking so much on the phone, it was just easier for him to be here," she said. "I'll tell you more about it later. Don't worry, we haven't started without you."

"Okay," I said, not knowing how else to respond. "You look amazing by the way." She did too. Her new dress was skimpy, clung to her body and showed a lot of leg. It was borderline slutty given what Jen normally wore, although I'd seen Allie wearing even more revealing dresses. She wore hose and high heels. Her hair and makeup were perfect. She looked like a super model!

I was used to Jen making an effort to look extra good. She'd done it for me – going out on the town or for work events – but mostly to present the two of us in the most favorable light. But I knew tonight, her motivation was to look as fuckable as possible for Scott. And god she looked good!

"I like this color," I said touching her fingers. I could tell she got a manicure today as the polish on her nails was smooth and perfect.

"I got a pedi too," she told me. Then with a giggle, she added "And a wax."

I got a lump in my throat, knowing she was talking about a Brazilian. Jen had gone all out to look sexy for Scott.

Jen saw the little plastic bag in my hand. "Bedroom," she whispered to me. I nodded and went into our bedroom with the condoms. I put them on the nightstand, on Jen's side. We had talked about this earlier. The action would be in our bedroom rather than the smaller bedroom where Joey used to sleep. That double bed was too small. Our king size bed was much better. And I admit, the thought of another man taking Jen in the bed we slept it got my cuckold fires going.

When I returned, Jen was in the kitchen working on dinner. Scott was with her, chopping vegetables. When she saw me, Jen said, "Mike can you be bartender?"

Bartender is my normal job when we have people over. I play bartender and Jen entertains our guests in the kitchen. It's probably how most couples do it. But as I watched Jen standing side-by-side with Scott, merrily chatting and laughing as they cooked dinner, I felt like he was the husband and I the guest. I felt like a third wheel. It was a classic cuckold moment and it excited me, but I felt left out.

Surprisingly, it was Scott who brought me into the conversation. We talked about a wide range of subjects, from sports to politics to movies. Scott seemed to go with whatever I wanted to talk about, and he had interesting points of view without being overbearing. I never felt like he was trying to take over the conversation. If anything, I was talking more than him. Scott has a quick wit and I found myself laughing at his jokes. Scott wasn't anything like the loud arrogant prick I'd come to know. He was actually quite pleasant and affable, and I found myself relaxing and having fun.

Jen noticed and she gave me a friendly "I told you so" grin. When we had a moment of privacy, I admitted "Okay, he's not so bad."

Jen squeezed my arm appreciatively, clearly happy I was warming up to Scott. "He just takes time getting used to," she told me.

Dinner was wonderful. Jen doesn't cook often but when she tries she can make really healthy, delicious meals.

Afterward we moved to our TV room. Scott sat on the sofa and Jen sat next to him. That surprised me because for the last 10 years, Jen always sat next to me. Of course, it wasn't that way at Stowe last weekend, but people always mingle at a party. This was different, this was in our home. For the first time in 10 years, Jen sat next to another man instead of me. My stomach was churning but I didn't say anything. That's why we were here after all.

Our hands were empty so I took another drink order. It took me a few minutes because Jen wanted a Cosmo and I had to go into our little pantry for cranberry juice. When I got back with the drinks, Jen and

Scott were looking at the pictures on our shelf. "That's your mom and sister?" Scott asked.

"Yes. At Cape Cod last summer."

"Your sister's a knock out. So's your mom. How old is she?" Scott asked.

"Fifty five," Jen said.

"Damn, she's a good looking woman. She looks ten years younger." Scott noticed me there and grinned. "You're a lucky man Mike. Your lady's got good genes." Jen smiled at Scott, then at me, then at Scott again.

"And these are your folks, Mike?" Scott asked looking at more pictures after I handed out the new drinks.

"Yes," I told him.

Scott got to our wedding pictures. "Jen, you were a beautiful bride," he said.

"Thank you," she said.

"And a handsome groom," Scott said, grinning at me.

I smiled awkwardly.

We had a big book of photos and Jen pulled it from the shelf. Scott sat on the sofa and again Jen sat next to him. I took the seat across from them.

"That's Per Se," Jen said pointing at a picture. "Right after Mike proposed."

"Per Se? Nice," Scott said. "So how did Mike propose?"

"Well, Mike ordered a bottle of champagne, and then he got up all of a sudden and said he had to talk to the maître de. Well, I knew something was up, because he sweet talked me all the way in the cab."

"Sweet talked?" Scott said, giving us both a friendly grin.

"Yeah, you know, telling me how much he loved me, how much I meant to him," Jen said, grinning at Scott. They had our photo album on their laps, and they were sitting so close their legs touched. "Then he came back and got on one knee, and I was thinking, wow, like, this is really happening, I need to take this moment in."

"Sounds really special," Scott said. "Were you nervous Mike?"

"No, more like anxious," I said.

"Oh come on, Mike," Jen said with a laugh. Then she looked at Scott again and said, "He was nervous, I could tell."

"I was nervous about saying it right, the way I rehearsed and not screwing it up. Okay, fine, I was nervous."

Scott and Jen laughed. Then Mike said "Well, who wouldn't be nervous? It's a monumental life moment."

Jen and Scott both smiled encouragingly at me. Their smiles felt patronizing to me. I didn't get it. Why was Jen talking about how I proposed to her, to the man she was about to fuck? And why did I still feel like a third wheel even as we looked at our family photo album?

Every time in the past when we looked at our family photo album with guests, I felt really close to her, and even as she narrated the photos to our guests, she constantly smiled into my eyes. This time though, it seemed like Scott was number 1 in her attentions, and I was a third wheel. She was smiling into his eyes instead of mine. Every second this went on, it was like a big hand gripping and squeezing my heart.

"Were you surprised?" Scott asked, seemingly to both of us, but looking at Jen.

"Well, by then we had talked about marriage," Jen said. "I mean, you knew I was going to say yes, right Mike?"

"Well, I guess, but you're never fully sure. I wasn't taking it for granted," I said.

The conversation moved from how I proposed, to our wedding, and then to our honeymoon. Even though they were talking about us, about the most special days in our lives, the conversation was between Jen and Scott with me continuing to feel like a third wheel and fighting to get a word in.

"So I bet you wore something special under your wedding dress," Scott said with a grin at Jen.

"You betcha mister," Jen said grinning at me, and then turning back and smiling at Scott. "Something old, something new."

"Let me guess," Scott said, grinning at me, then at Jen again. "A new bustier. New stockings." Each time, Jen nodded her pretty head. "So what was old?"

"Kinda lame, but Sophie – she was my maid of honor – she loaned me the garter she wore at her wedding," Jen told him.

"Allie wasn't your maid of honor?" Scott asked, knowing Allie was Jen's best friend and they were really tight.

"I've known Sophie since the second grade," Jen said. "We're still good friends, but yeah, Allie's my best friend now. You know how those things go."

"You bet I know," Scott said with another grin at her. "I bet it was a sick reception."

"It was the best!" Jen gushed. Even though she was talking about our wedding, she was smiling into Scott's eyes. "We danced all night! Mike paid for it. My parents couldn't afford to pay."

Scott looked at me and smiled. "Your man's Mr. Responsible," he said.

"You bet he is," Jen said, smiling at me too. Again I felt like they were patronizing me. Throwing me a crumb here and there to make me feel like I was in the conversation, when in fact it was just between them. And what did he mean by "Mr. Responsible"?

"So high heels too?" Scott asked.

"Pretty white satin heels," Jen said, raising her leg as if showing off the bridal high heel (but of course she was wearing one of her new Jimmy Choo high heels). "Only two inches though. High heels hurt my feet, and with all the dancing ...."

"But these are what, four inches?"

"Yep," Jen said, her slim, shapely leg still extended. "I'm getting used to them."

"Sexy. Your legs are amazing," Scott said as looked at her shapely, stockinged leg. Then he looked into her face and they smiled into each other's eyes. After a moment, he turned to me and said, "So Jenny's changing for the better, right Mike?"

I nodded. I hated the way he called her Jenny. Her name was Jen, not Jenny.

But Jen didn't seem to mind. She laughed and said, "I'm changing for the better?"

Scott grinned at her and said, "It's always better when a hot chick wears fuck me pumps."

"Oh god," Jen said, laughing again and punching his arm.

My head felt like it was going to explode. My heart felt like it was breaking.

Scott pulled out a couple joints. I looked at them warily. I didn't want to get high and wasted again, like at Stowe.

But Jen looked excited to get high again. Scott lit up and took a drag. He handed the joint to Jen and she took a long drag, inhaling the sweet smoke deep into her lungs. She rolled her head back as the warmth spread through. "That's really good," she gushed, passing the joint back to Scott.

"You look sexy as hell with your lips on a cigarette," Scott admired. Her brownish-red lipstick now coated the end of the joint. "Right Mike?" he added, grinning at me.

"Typical men," Jen said with a grin, looking at me and then at Scott again. He took a long drag. "Yeah, that's definitely good shit," he said.

"Weed always gets me horny," Jen said with a laugh.

"Then next time I'll bring more joints," Scott said, and they both laughed.

Weed got her horny? I thought. *Why had she never told me that?*

Scott offered the joint to her again. "Ready to get hornier?" he asked with a grin.

Jen grinned back and was about to take it when she stopped and looked at me, as if remembering I was there. "Mike baby, do you want some?" she asked, offering the joint to me.

I really didn't. But I didn't want to be a party poop. "Sure," I said. Jen handed me the joint and I took a drag. Not a big one. Just enough to say I did.

We passed the joint around again. Then I noticed our drinks were empty. I asked, "Another round?"

"What do you think Scotty?" Jen asked. I noticed she was deferring to him, asking him instead of me. It bothered me of course.

"Maybe one more," Scott said. When I got up to make the drinks, he said "Thanks buddy."

While in the kitchen, I heard Scott asked Jen, "So thong or g-string?"

"You know I wear thongs," Jen said with a giggle. She sounded like a silly young schoolgirl talking to a boy she was majorly crushing on. She sounded high too.

"I meant under your wedding dress," Scott said with a grin.

"Oh my god," she said with another laugh. "G-string." As I mixed the drinks, I couldn't believe she was talking to Scott about the lingerie she wore on our wedding day.

"I bet you were a smoking hot bride," Scott said.

"You've got the pictures," Jen said with a happy smile.

"I mean under your dress," Scott said.

"Oh," Jen said, and they both laughed.

"Now?"

"Now what?" Jen said.

"What are you wearing under this?" he asked, touching her skirt.

"I told you," she said. "A thong."

"Not a g-string? You don't like floss up your ass?" he joked, and they both laughed.

"And?"

Jen giggled. "Stockings," she said.

"Not pantyhose?"

"I think I'm over pantyhose," Jen said. With a teasing grin, she added "Boys like stockings."

"I'm a boy," Scott said with a grin back at her.

"I've figured that out," she said with a laugh.

"Mike's not a boy?" Scott asked. This was him being a dick.

"Of course he is," Jen said immediately. She looked nervously at the kitchen. "But you know ... stockings are harder to wear. And Mike is so sweet. He always thinks about me first."

"Sure, I get it," Scott said. "So what else under your dress? Bra?"

"You mean under my wedding dress?"

"Sure."

"I wore a bustier, and that doubled as a bra," Jen said.

"I wish I'd seen you. As a bride," Scott said, smiling admiringly at her. "I can look at the pictures, but I wish I could've seen you in person. I bet every guy there wished you were his bride."

"I don't know about that," Jen said, looking down demurely. She was practically blushing. It was clear she loved the compliment.

"So what about now? No bra?"

"That's right. Can't you tell?"

"I can actually," he said looking at her chest.

"You're into that," Jen said. It was half question, half statement.

"Yeah, I am," Scott admitted with a chuckle. "You're really something."

"Am I?" Jen said, clearly flattered.

"Yeah, you are."

When I walked back into the TV room, I stopped in my tracks. Jen and Scott were kissing.

I stood in the corner so as not to be noticed. I wanted to see how far it would go. Would Jen pull out Scott's cock out of his pants and start sucking it right then and there?

In my semi-stoned state, part of me was thinking, "Just go for it Jen, let me see you do it, pull it out and let's see you suck Scott's big fat cock. Let me see you sit on it. Let me see him fuck your brains out." I was being childish and vindictive, but that was how I was feeling at that moment.

But then Scott pulled away and whispered something in Jen's ear. She frowned and whispered something back. He moved his lips closer to her ear and whispered something more. Jen seemed reluctant, but eventually nodded her head in agreement.

Then Jen stood up and walked into the kitchen. She walked right past me but didn't say anything. She looked nervous and appeared to be forcing herself not to look at me.

I put the drinks on the table and sat down, not sure what was going on. I realized a moment later that Jen left the room so Scott and I could talk privately.

Scott moved closer to me, and said, "Hey bro, Jenny and I were talking, and I think we're going to go to the other room for a bit, okay?"

"What?" I said, not understanding. I knew the "other room" was our bedroom. But what did he mean? They were going into the bedroom and leaving me out here? And he and Jen talked about this? When? Just now, or earlier today?

In a reasonable voice, Scott said, "This scene is new for all of us. I think the first time, you know, with you watching, it'll be better if Jenny and I are alone for a bit. Just at the start. You get it, right?"

"This is your idea?" I asked, looking incredulously at him.

Scott shook his head and said, "It's more like, we both came to the same way of thinking. It's kind of weird with someone watching. No offense, it's just new for everyone. So just let us get started. Say, give us an hour. Maybe two. Something like that. Enough time for us to get going. Then you can come in and watch all you want."

I was shocked. This was our game. Me and Jen. *Our* game. And she was excluding me?

And the way he said, "then you can come in *and watch all you want*." He was making it sound like I was a freak. A sicko. *He* was the one sleeping around with another man's wife. *He* was the one committing all kinds of sins, not me.

When Jen walked back in, she saw me and Scott talking. She looked over at Scott. As though reading her mind, he said "We talked, it's all good."

Jen said, "It is?" She had that nervous look on her pretty face.

She turned from Scott to me. "You're okay baby?" she asked me.

I felt in shock, my head spinning. I found myself saying, "Yes. I'm good."

Jen smiled appreciatively at me. She asked, "Do you mind if we take the second joint? There's still most of the first one left if you want it."

"What?" I said. I was numb and didn't understand what she was saying.

"The rest of the first joint," she said. "It's on the coffee table. If you want any. The lighter's right there."

"Okay," I said, still feeling numb. And stunned.

Scott stood up and walked over to her. I stood up too. For the first time I noticed Jen holding a bucket of ice full of beers. "Do you want me to get you a Highland Park?" she asked me.

I looked at the table. I'd poured myself a glass of wine. Jen's Cosmo was there too, along with a beer for Scott. Jen seemed not to notice, or remember I'd gotten another round for us all. Before I could say anything, she put the beers down and said "Here, I'll get you one." She poured me a Highland Park scotch with a couple ice cubes. After handing it to me, she said "So you'll be okay?"

"Yeah, sure," I said.

"The joint's on the table," she reminded me again.

"Okay," I said.

Then Jen hugged me. "I love you baby," she whispered in my ear. I told her I loved her too. Then she picked up the second joint and walked back to Scott. He picked up the bucket of beers and a few cut up limes and put his arm around her. I watched them walk into the master bedroom, Scott's arm around my wife. They closed the door behind them.

I felt stunned. What had just happened? I was out here, and Scott was partying with my wife. In my bedroom. How had the evening shifted so quickly to this?

I heard music from the bedroom. Jen had put on one of her playlists on her iPhone. I took the wine, Cosmo and beer to the kitchen. I poured them out, leaving the discards in the sink. Then I walked back to the chair. The chair faced the bedroom door. I sat in it and looked at the closed door. I didn't touch the scotch or joint.

I sat motionless for a long time. My heart was broken and my cock ached in my pants. How was that combination even possible? I couldn't help myself. I moved close to the bedroom door. Apartment walls in New York City are thin.

I heard whispers and kissing. A lot of kissing. The rustling of clothes. I heard moans. I distinctly heard Jen say, "God you're big." It came out like a groan.

Later I heard her say, "you feel so good inside me." She said that a lot to him. Jen squealed and grunted and moaned. He was fucking her really good. She never made sounds like that with me.

I heard when she came. She moaned, "Oh god you're making me cum!" Her moans became urgent and helpless. I heard her gasp "Oh gaaaaaaaawd!" A little later I heard her say "Oh my god that was so freaking amazing!"

Then I heard more kissing and whispering. After a bit it started up again. I think he made her cum again. Then I heard Scott cum. I think maybe they switched positions and Jen got on top. "That feels really good," he moaned. "Do that. Yeah. Do that. Don't stop."

I knew what she was doing. She was squeezing her pussy as she moved up and down on his shaft. She did it with me and it never failed to make me cum.

His moans became more urgent and constant. I heard shuffling on the bed as he put her back into the missionary position so he could really fuck the shit out of her. Or maybe onto her hands and knees. His moans became raw and primal, and I heard the bed slam against the wall over and over again.

"I'm fucking cumming!" he cried.

"Oh yeah cum in me baby cum inside me!" Jen urged him.

I heard a massive long primal moan from him, and then another, and another. He was cumming inside my wife. I prayed to God she'd made him wear a condom. I prayed to God the condom hadn't fallen off or ripped.

I looked down and saw I'd cum on my hand. I hadn't even realized it but I'd taken out my cock and masturbated as they fucked.

I returned to the sofa, expecting Jen to come get me. I didn't know if tonight was over. But even if not, I expected she'd come out and check on me. I wanted a few moments alone with her. I needed to hold her, I needed a little reassurance from her that it'd just been raw meaningless sex with Scott, that she still loved *me*, that she was *still mine*.

But she didn't come out of the bedroom. Not 5 minutes later, or 10, or 30 minutes. I silently walked back to the bedroom door. They were laughing and talking inside. I heard the opening of beers, the clinking of bottles, the smell of weed. They were best buds, in the afterglow of incredible sex and orgasms. They were partying.

I went back to the sofa. I waited. Surely, she'd come out to see how I was doing, right? They were in *our* bed. Pictures of us back in college, our wedding, our life together, they were all over our bedroom. There were tons of reminders of us in there, *of me* in there. She couldn't forget I was out here all alone and waiting, right? She'd come and see how I was doing, right?

But she didn't come out. Instead, I heard sounds of sex again. They were going at it again. Scott had Jenny Paige Andrews in his arms, and he wasn't letting her get away. Despite myself I beat off again. I shot my jizz onto the sofa next to me. Then I put my head in my hands and did my best to keep from crying.

I managed to pull myself together. I cleaned the sofa. Finally I reached for the Highland Park and took a big gulp.

Maybe I dozed. I don't know. At some point I felt Jen softly shake my shoulder. "Hey you," she softly said. She wore a tender smile and jostled my hair. "Are you okay?"

"Yeah, sure," I said. I wasn't going to let her know how pathetic I was. How close I had come to crying. The clock said 1am. They'd been together for hours.

"We're almost done, okay?" she said rubbing my arm.

"Yeah, sure," I said again. I looked at her. Her hair was tussled and her make up gone. She looked radiant. She was wearing a shirt. I didn't recognize it at first. Then it hit me. She was wearing Scott's shirt.

She wasn't even wearing one of my shirts. She was wearing Scott's fucking shirt.

Jen got three big glasses of water. I watched her as she filled the glasses. Her legs and feet were bare. Somewhere along the way she lost the heels and stockings. All she had on was Scott's shirt.

Jen gave me one of the glasses. "I want you to drink this," she told me. Then she stroked my cheek. "We're almost done," she said again. When I nodded, she smiled at me. Then she walked back into the bedroom.

Sounds of sex came from the bedroom. I looked at the joint. What the hell. I smoked the entire thing and got high. It helped some as I listened to the bed shake and Jen's constant moans. My cock was hard. I stroked myself and came fast again. Despite my despair, my orgasm was incredibly intense.

I must have passed out. When I woke it was past 7am. All was quiet. I approached the bedroom. I didn't hear anything. I slowly opened the door. They were asleep, both of them nude. Their naked bodies were tangled together. Scott was on his back. His arm was around her, and she was snuggled into him. Her head was in the crook of his arm, her long lush blonde hair covering his chest. One of her slim, shapely legs was over his, her hand on his chest.

I sat back down on the sofa. I wasn't able to move. My heart was broken. My worst fears had come true. Again, I forced myself not to cry.

A little later I heard stirring in the bedroom. Then moans. They were fucking again. I listened as Scott made my wife cum again.

Finally, the bedroom door opened. It was Jen. She came over to me. She looked tired but beautiful as always. She was wearing her fluffy cotton robe. At least she wasn't wearing his shirt again.

She sat next to me, looking up into my face. She could tell I was an emotional mess. "I'm sorry. We passed out. That's why I didn't get you."

I nodded dumbly, feeling in a stupor.

She reached for my hand. She squeezed my hand, but I didn't squeeze back. I was numb. I felt dead inside.

She sat next to me, looking at me concerned. Scott came out of the bedroom. He was dressed. He had the decency to look embarrassed and maybe even guilty. "Sorry buddy, we passed out last night," he said, repeating the same story as Jen. But what about "just give us a couple of hours to get going"? What about that?

He moved to the door, motioning towards Jen. "I'll be right back," she said to me. She squeezed my hand and then walked over to Scott in the foyer.

"He's really upset," I heard Jen whisper.

"He'll be okay," Scott assured her. "I had a great time."

Jen didn't answer but I heard them kiss. "See you Monday," Scott said.

"Yeah, Monday," Jen said. I heard them kiss again. A few seconds later the door opened and closed. He was gone.

CHAPTER 9

Jen sat next to me, looking at my face. She looked concerned. She leaned her head on my shoulder. When I didn't push her away, she put her arms around me. "I'm sorry. I passed out. I swear. Too much weed, I guess," she said with a cautious smile.

She looked into my eyes. "Will you say something?" she implored.

I hurt a lot. But I didn't want to show it. I probably already looked pathetic to her. I didn't want to lose more of her respect. "I'll be okay," I said, putting on a brave face.

She looked at me, doubt on her pretty face. But she didn't press. She hugged me. It felt good. I felt my insides coming alive again. I wrapped my arms around her, and hugged back.

We got in the shower together. We soaped each other. She winced when I soaped her pussy and clit. "It's kinda sore," she said. No doubt he'd fucked her raw. I soaped her more gently. "That feels good," she said.

She got on her knees. She took my cock into her mouth. Within moments, I came in her mouth.

Jen changed the sheets. Then we got into bed and she leaned into my shoulder, into the crook of my arm. I put my arm around her, and her blonde hair draped over my chest. She put her arm on my chest and one leg over mine. Jen must've been exhausted because she fell asleep immediately.

Our snuggling reminded me of what I saw earlier, of Jen and Scott asleep, their bodies tangled together. Probably we looked the same now as they looked then. A wave of angst washed over me as I remembered what I saw. But I was rock hard too. I was so excited I was on the verge of a shaking attack. Somehow, I was able to relax and I fell asleep too.

When I woke up the sun was going down. I realized I was breathing hard. Jen was awake. She was looking at me. She had my cock in her hand and was slowly stroking me. "Hi sleepyhead," she said smiling at me.

Jen got on top of me and guided my cock into her. She rode me. Then we switched positions, and I fucked her missionary. Because I'd cum so much I was able to last. We fucked for maybe 15 minutes. I noticed Jen didn't moan or groan or cry out like last night with Scott. Not even close.

"You're still upset," Jen said after we were done. We were on our backs next to each other in bed. The sun was below the horizon now.

"I don't have the right to be upset?" I asked, sarcasm and bitterness in my voice.

"You have a right," Jen said. "I passed out—."

"I'm not upset because you passed out!" I said angrily. "That's like #25 on my upset list! Number 1, why'd you exclude me?!"

"Mike, please, don't yell at me, I can't think when you yell at me," Jen implored, putting her hands over her ears. That was how Jen was. She wasn't confrontational. She hated when someone was mad at her. She hated when someone yelled at her.

"Then tell me why you excluded me!" I insisted.

"I don't know. We talked about it. Scott suggested it."

"And you agreed?!" I said incredulously.

"Mike please," Jen pleaded. "Can't we talk without yelling?"

I closed my eyes and counted to 10, trying to calm myself. "Okay, I'm not yelling," I finally said in a more normal voice.

Jen looked at me and nodded. She said, "I talked to Scott yesterday. About what would happen. I got kinda freaked about you watching. I thought you'd see us together and get upset."

"That's my choice," I said, barely able to keep the anger from my voice.

"I know, I know, we were just talking," Jen said soothingly.

"Why were you talking to him anyway?" I asked.

"Mike ...," Jen said imploringly. "This is our game – *our* game—but we're playing with Scott. He's part of this. It's not fair to ask me not to talk to him."

It upset me, but I knew she was right. "Okay, okay," I said, giving in on that one.

"Anyways ...," she continued hesitantly, as if judging her words carefully to avoid getting me angry again. "Scotty said maybe you'd like it."

"What?" I said, not understanding.

"Scott's good with people. That's why he's good with advertising," Jen explained. "Scotty said maybe it would push your cuckold buttons, if we told you to wait outside."

"And you went along with it?" I said incredulously.

"Mike baby, the door wasn't locked," Jen said pleadingly. "This is *your* house. *Your* bed. I'm *your* wife. You could've come in anytime you wanted. We waited for you. But you didn't come in. So I figured Scotty was right. It did push your buttons."

I stared at her disbelievingly. "Do you realize how upset I got?" I asked.

"But it got you hot right? Did you play with yourself? How many times did you cum?"

I tried to remember. I wasn't sure. "Once or twice. Maybe three times," I admitted. "But I don't like you scheming against me."

"I'm not scheming against you baby. I'm trying to figure you out. Scott suggested it. I went with it because it helped my anxieties too. But you were welcome to join us anytime."

"I didn't feel welcome," I said.

Jen grinned at me. "Now you sound like a baby," she said with a pretend pout. When I scowled at her, she giggled and tickled me. I tickled her back, and then we were rolling and laughing on the bed. Then we were fucking again.

After, we got Chinese delivery for dinner and ate fried rice and steamed vegetables while watching the Mets. God they suck.

"It bothered me seeing you wearing his shirt," I said.

Jen sighed, resting her head on my shoulder. "This is weird for me too," she said. "I'm your wife, but I'm with Scotty."

"So you wore his shirt on purpose?"

"I wore his shirt because it felt right," Jen said. "I just freaking came with him. I was cold. Putting on his shirt felt right."

"So there are emotions, it's not just sex," I said challengingly.

"Mike ... yeah," Jen said with more than a little exasperation. "That's why it's Scott. We're friends. I don't want one-night stands. We talked about this. I don't want to feel like a slut. I want it to be a friend. So yeah, there are feelings. Is that terrible? I mean, we talked about this."

"... no, it's not terrible," I said, my voice dry. Jen noticed the hoarseness of my voice. She gave me a crooked grin and said, "Is this turning you on?"

I hesitated, then said "Emotions make it more intense."

"So you like it?"

"I like it and hate it," I said with an embarrassed laugh.

Jen reached into my pants. I was wearing sweats. She found me hard. She wrapped her hand around my shaft and slowly stroked me. "So if I fell in love with Scotty, that would really get you hot," she said with a grin on her pretty face.

She felt my body tense. She quickly said "I'm not gonna. I'm just asking. I'm just trying to figure you out."

Breathing hard, I said, "I think ultimately, the cuckold fantasy is about the risk of losing your wife to another man." With an embarrassed laugh, I admitted, "I have no idea why that turns me on."

Still with a lopsided grin on her face, she said "Hey, I'm the freak girl who gets turned on by rape. So I can't judge."

"Yeah," I said, and we shared a half laugh.

"Mike honey," Jen said. "You'll never lose me to Scott. But it might feel that way sometimes. Do you want to explore that with me? As part of our game?"

"How will we do that?" I asked.

Jen shrugged. "I don't know," she said. "He'll still be my bud. We'll hang out. Sometimes we'll have nights like this."

I felt a wave of cuckold angst wash over me. It churned my insides. But tasted so delicious.

I was breathing really hard now. But I still had my misgivings.

"Can we just see how it goes?" I asked. I didn't want to commit. I didn't want to move too fast.

But I didn't shut the door either.

Jen rubbed my arm and gave me an understanding smile. Then, pulling back her long blonde hair, she pulled down my sweats and went down on me.

CHAPTER 10

I watched Scott fuck Jen the next weekend. Friday night actually. Before that though, Scott and I met for a drink, to talk about things. Jen said it was Scott's idea. We met at a sports bar and they had the Mets on. Scott was a Mets fan too. We commiserated about how trading Seaver was the low point in Mets history, and how Gooden and Strawberry had been such painful disappointments.

It would be too much to say I liked Scott. Even when he was pleasant, as now, there was still the air of arrogant macho asshole about him. I didn't like him. I probably borderline hated him. But maybe at least now I didn't despise him.

As if reading my mind, Scott said, "You hate me, don't you?"

When I shrugged, he chuckled. "Okay, I get that. I'm fucking your lady, so of course you hate me. Actually, I respect that. Better truth than bullshit."

I looked around. Luckily no one was around to hear our conversation. "Just treat her with respect," I told him.

Scott laughed and said, "Bro, believe me, Jenny wants me to treat her like a slut." Seeing my glare at him, he said "Calm down, Jenny and I are buddies. But look, there's a reason she's fucking me. Pretty obvious. She's not getting what she needs from you, so she's looking other places."

I narrowed my eyes and balled my hands into fists. I was this close to punching him. Scott saw my fury. He frowned and said, "Calm down bro. I'm just telling the truth. We all saw it at work. We talked about it. Jenny needed laid big time, because she wasn't getting it from you. I'm just being honest. You're lucky she's not cheating on you. Maybe she is."

"Jen would never cheat on me!" I hissed at him.

"Okay, whatever," Scott said with a shrug. "You believe that if you want. Me, I've seen a lot of horny married chicks like Jen. I've fucked my share too."

I glared at Scott. Clearly, he had no qualms with fucking married woman, maybe breaking up their marriages. I changed my mind, maybe I *did* despise him.

Scott either didn't notice my glare or didn't care. He said, "One chick, her husband's like you. He liked watching me fucking his wife. So I've been around this block before."

I raised an eyebrow at that. I wanted to ask questions, but I knew that would be a mistake so I kept my mouth shut.

"A couple things we need to get straight," Scott told me, getting down to business. "I don't do threesomes. Not with other dudes anyway. I'm good with MFF but not MMF. You get me? That dude I just talked about? One time, me and his wife are fucking. She starts to cum and he kisses her. So his head is between me and his wife's face. All I can see as I'm banging her pussy is his balding head. Mike, that's fucked up. That's not how I roll. So watch if you want, but from a distance. We good on that bro?"

I nodded. I tried to act normal but my heart was pounding and my dick rock hard.

"Another thing," Scott continued. "When I'm with Jenny, she's with me. I'm saying, don't go alpha on me. I don't need the drama, and she doesn't want it either, believe me."

I nodded again. I was so worked up I didn't trust myself to say anything.

"Okay then, glad we got that worked out," Scott said, grinning at me. He finished his beer then stood up. "You'll get this?" he said, motioning to the bill. I nodded. He grinned and said, "See you Friday bro." Then he left. I stayed at the bar, waiting for my hard-on to go down.

My head was spinning. Scott just laid down rules about my wife, and I gave into all of it. It hurt my pride. It hurt my manhood. I felt like my claim over my wife was slipping away. But god I was so hot I was barely able to avoid trembling.

Scott said I wasn't satisfying Jen, to the point she probably had been close to cheating on me. That maybe she *had* cheated on me already. Was that possible? She certainly had the opportunity with all my traveling and working late. And I knew I had been neglecting her.

I decided not to confront Jen about it. It wouldn't be fair as I had no evidence. I would just keep my eyes open and confront her if I saw something.

———◉———

Jen bought another dress for Friday night. She told me she wanted something new to wear for Scott. I didn't understand that, because there were lots of clothes in her closet that Scott had never seen before. But Jen was so excited about shopping for a new outfit, that I didn't have the heart to stop her.

There was a pain in my gut – that was becoming a familiar feeling – seeing Jen so excited about seeing another man. Getting all glammed up with doing her hair, her makeup, buying a new dress and high heels. I liked the new additions to her wardrobe. Everything was way sexier than the "fashionable yet conservative" clothes she'd worn the last few years. It was like wrapping a gift though. You spend all that time wrapping it, and then in 2 seconds the wrapping was off. I got an ache in my heart (and an erection in my pants) thinking about Scott unwrapping my wife.

What made it extra hard was Jen saw Scott all the time, since they worked together. They didn't work on the same projects, but their offices were on the same floor, and they talked every day. They texted too, often at home when she was sitting beside me on the sofa or in bed. I wondered if people at her work gossiped that Jen was having sex with

Scott? That possibility kept my dick hard (as if I needed anything else to keep my dick hard). It turned me on that people might think that Jen was fucking Scott behind my back. I guess it pushed my cuckold buttons.

Friday was a replay of last Friday. Jen and Scott cooked while I played bartender. The conversation was mostly between Jen and Scott while I looked on. They were so into each other, it truly felt like they were the couple and I was the guest they invited over for dinner. More than once I had to look at Jen's wedding rings – my rings – to reassure myself that she was my wife and we were just playing the game.

One time I came into the kitchen and found Jen and Scott locked in an embrace, kissing. I could tell they were tonguing each other by the way their cheeks moved. I stood back and watched. It was the most erotic sight, but god, it hurt. To see my wife kissing another man, it broke my heart even while my dick was hard as a rock.

I cleared my throat and they pulled away. They were both panting, their faces flushed. Jen's nipples were hard (they were denting the fabric of her new dress), and Scott had an obscenely huge tent in his pants. Jen came over to me with a weak smile on her pretty face. She rubbed my chest and gave me a quick kiss, and whispered "I love you." Then she went back to the stove to finish cooking, Scott beside her, like nothing had happened.

After dinner in the TV room, I found them kissing again. This time was more passionate as they were groping each other too. They were like horny teenagers, unable to keep their hands off each other. Scott kissed down Jen's chin to her neck. She rolled her head back and moaned as he kissed her neck. Her neck is incredible sensitive, especially behind her ear. Scott's hands moved down her body and he pulled up her dress. I saw Jen was wearing lace topped stockings and a garter belt.

When had she begun wearing garter belts with real silk stockings? For that matter, when had she begun wearing thigh high stockings? Jen had always worn pantyhose, and that was when she wore any hose at all. It amazed me at how she had changed so much in such a short period of time.

Scott pushed his hand into Jen's panties and fingered her. Jen writhed as he worked on her, moaning and groaning. Jen must've been really worked up because within moments she came. Her body arched up off the sofa, and it was a lewd sight to see her long stockinged legs spread open with Scott's hand down her panties, her body shuddering with an orgasm.

Afterwards, Jen giggled as she pushed down her dress and pressed her knees together. She seemed embarrassed that she had let herself go like that, especially when she looked over at me.

Jen was still in Scott's arms. His erection was huge, it looked like a python in his pants. Jen's leg was partially bent over his, so I knew she could feel it. Scott whispered something to Jen and she whispered something back, and then they got up. They were holding hands. Jen squeezed Scott's hand and then they began moving towards our bedroom. "We're going to the bedroom," she told me in a soft voice.

"Am I allowed this time?" I said. I made it sound like a joke, but there was a touch of bitter resentfulness in my voice. Jen didn't answer, but she gently stroked my cheek. It was like she was reminding me that I could have watched last time because the door had been unlocked.

Like last time, Jen went to our bar (it's actually a small cart) and poured me a Highland Park with a couple cubes of ice. She gave it to me. "You're good baby?" she asked.

"Yeah," I said.

"Want me to turn the TV on? To the Mets game?"

"I'll do it," I said.

"So you're good?" she asked again.

"Yeah, I'm good," I assured her. Jen smiled at me and then joined Scott in our bedroom. She closed the door partway, leaving it open about a foot. She was inviting me to enter and watch, if I wanted.

I sat on the sofa, unable to move. It was hard to describe the anguish – the heart wrenching anguish—knowing my wife was not completely mine anymore. But there it was, right in front me. Scott knew he had a claim on my wife's body. He could kiss her, fondle her, make her cum, anytime he wanted, even right in front of me. My wife wasn't exclusively mine anymore.

It wasn't just the sex either. Jen's relationship with Scott was blooming and she was having such a good time. She seemed to have a permanent smile plastered to her face. She got so excited, giddy even, when she knew she was going to see Scott. I knew it was NRE and this infatuation wouldn't last forever, but still it caused me major angst. I'd read stories and threads, probably thousands, and I knew I should let the jealously go. I had Jen's heart and mind and that should have been enough. But human nature was what it was, and the reality of it was that you have these feelings and you just can't will them away, no matter how hard you tried.

I sipped the scotch as I heard sounds of sex coming from the bedroom. Finally, I got up and went into the bedroom. What I saw will haunt me for the rest of my life.

Jen and Scott were both naked (although she still wore the garter belt, stockings and high heels). She was on top, riding his cock. Even though I knew Scott was big I was still shocked by his size. Thick and hugely long. Jen was going slow, clearly adjusting to his size. I could see how stretched her outer lips are. You could see how the muscles of her inner thighs were straining – like, the look when a woman is trying to pull her legs together but can't. Jen was really struggling to accommodate Scott's manhood. Her long, lush, slightly wavy blonde hair was hanging down over her face and breasts, and her hands were firmly planted on his chest, as she balanced herself on his long, thick shaft.

I felt like I was going to have a heart attack, that's how hard my heart was beating against my chest. But god I was so hard. My dick hurt from so much blood pumping through it. Another man was inside my wife! Yes, I knew it happened last week, but I didn't see it. Now it was playing out in front of me. My wife had another man's cock inside her!

I staggered into the loveseat facing our bed as all at once, the reality of it hit me. Jen was no longer all mine. Her pretty pussy was no longer all mine. Another man was taking her. Our lives would never be the same again. Once another man has fucked your wife, you can't take it back.

The sight of Jen's pretty face was amazing. There was strain there from taking something so big. But mostly, the look of pure, unadulterated lust in her eyes. It was one of the greatest things I've ever experienced. She looked so beautiful at that moment. The image actually helped me deal with the angst. It reminded me of why I pushed her into this 'game' in the first place. I was seeing her experience pleasure I could never give her, and I loved it. I loved Jen more at that moment than ever before. I was so happy for her.

I took out my cock and stroked myself. Almost immediately I came. My ejaculation was so powerful my jism landed on the rug a couple of feet from where I was sitting.

Jen didn't notice as I orgasmed. Maybe she didn't realize I was in the room. At that moment, she had worked all of Scott's cock into her and was beginning to ride him. Her manicured fingernails dug into his chest as she moved up and down on his shaft.

Scott pulled Jen down to him and wrapped his arms around her. They kissed, moaning into the other's mouth, as she fucked herself on his big cock.

Then Scott took control. He rose up on his powerful legs and started hammering her. Jen whimpered and cried out. I'd never heard those sounds come from her lips before. Her moans and shrieks were constant now. I'd never seen her like this. Our sex had never been this way. This passionate.

This *primal*.

Suddenly Jen's body tensed and her back arched. She was cumming. The pointy toes of her high heels dug into the mattress. Jen rolled her head back and her lips parted into an O. She started wailing, low at first, and then louder and louder and finally ending into a scream. Her body shuddered violently, and then she rolled her head forward, her long blonde hair splashing onto Scott's muscular chest. "Oh gooooooood!" she screamed, so loud I'm sure the entire building heard her.

She collapsed onto Scott's chest, and he hugged her and stroked her hair. "Oh god oh god oh god," she breathlessly panted, over and over again.

Scott gave Jen a few moments to recover. Then he flipped her onto her hands and knees. He fucked her hard from behind. He growled with each powerful thrust, one hand gripping her hip, the other pushing down the back of her neck, fucking her so hard he was practically pushing her pretty face through the mattress. Clearly now that he'd gotten Jen off, this was all for his pleasure. She moaned and whimpered, her slender fingers with pink nail polish clawing at the sheets. "Oh shit, oh shit, oh shit," Jen moaned, and then she started screaming as she came again. "Oh god! Shit! God! OH GOD!!!!!!"

"I'M FUCKING CUMMING!" Scott growled, and then it was like time standing still. He pushed in deep, his head rolling back and his face contorted, and then his orgasm hit. He screamed "OH FUCK!" and then he was slamming Jen hard as he came inside her.

Both Jen and Scott collapsed onto the bed. They were breathing so hard I could hear their panting. Eventually Scott rolled off, pulling his cock from her. It seemed to take forever, that's how long he was, and when the big head pulled out there was an audible pop. I was relieved to see the condom still on, and it hadn't ripped. The reservoir bulb at the tip was full of his sperm. It was so heavy with sperm that it sagged down over his cockhead.

Scott took off the condom and wrapped it in some tissues. That's when he noticed me. My hand was around my half hard dick. I'd cum again so my hand was sticky with my own jizz.

Scott pulled Jen into his arms, and she cuddled into him. Scott grinned at me as he possessively held my wife, and as she cuddled into his arms and chest. I felt myself getting hard again.

They softly kissed, and then he whispered something to her. She hesitated, then nodded. She came over to me. She smiled at me, taking a moment to look at my cock. I was hard again, and my sticky hand was around my shaft. She didn't comment on it. Instead, she said, "Mike baby, do you mind if me and Scott have a little private time?"

I felt like she just stabbed me in the heart. But I understood. After passionate sex, lovers liked to cuddle and enjoy the moment. Still, I couldn't believe how insensitive Jen was to my feelings. As if reading my mind, she smiled reassuringly at me and gently brushed my cheek and said "Just a little while. I promise."

I managed a nod, and got up. Before I was even out the door, Jen was back in bed with Scott. I looked back at them and saw her snuggling in his arms and kissing him.

I cleaned up, then sat on the sofa. I heard whispers and giggles. The movement of sheets. Soft kisses and sweet nothings. Eventually I heard sounds of sex again. I walked to the door and looked in.

Jen was on her side this time, her shapely leg up, Scott fucking her from behind, his lips kissing her neck, his hands fondling her little tits and rubbing her nipples. It was a slower, deeper fuck this time.

Jen was facing me and her eyes were open, but they were glazed over with lust. I doubt she even saw me. Her lips were parted and there was a continuous soft moan coming from her. She had her cum face on again, that look of unbridled lust.

I watched as Jen came on his cock again. Her head rolled back and her back arched, and her toes curled (she'd lost the high heels but was still wearing the garter belt and stockings), and then she wailed a long, soulful moan as orgasmic pleasure seeped through her body.

Scott fucked her through her orgasm, and then he pulled her head back so she looked over her shoulder back at him. She kissed him as he came, his hips jerking as he ejaculated into my wife. I hoped to god he was wearing a condom.

Then there was movement of legs, and Jen was on top of Scott. They were panting into each other's face. Scott held Jen tight, and he tenderly kissed her face and whispered to her. She was looking into his eyes and nodding. I think he was inside her, their bodies still connected as they basked in the afterglow of their great sex and mutual orgasms.

I silently moved back to the sofa. I found their after-sex intimacy even more devastating than the sex itself. Yet, I was incredibly hard again. I reached into my pants and stroked myself. I had an incredible orgasm. I cleaned up and put on new boxers and pants.

Sometime later – it was about 2am – Jen came out with Scott. She was holding his hand, but at least she was wearing my old frat t-shirt. She squeezed my hand for a moment, smiled at me, then walked with Scott to the door. We'd agreed ahead of time that Scott wouldn't spend the night and I was glad and relieved she was living up to her promise.

I heard Jen kissed Scott, tell him how much fun she had, then I heard the door open and close. Jen came back to me and took my hand. She led me into our bedroom. Somehow, she had already changed the sheets. We snuggled, both of us too physically tired (and for me, emotionally tired too) for sex. What I really needed was my wife back, and she snuggled into my arms. We spooned and fell asleep without saying a word.

CHAPTER 11

It was the routine that helped me. And the reconnection after.
Jen hooked up with Scott every Friday. It was their "date" night. Because it was a regular schedule, I was able to mentally (and emotionally) psych myself up for it. He either didn't spend the night or left early Saturday morning, so I had the entire weekend to reconnect with her. That made the experience bearable for me. And also, I admit, enjoyable.

I was aroused all the time. *All the time.* And hard.

I thought Jen was the prettiest, hottest, sexiest girl on the planet. I was obsessed with her. She was constantly in my thoughts. When at work – especially when I was out of town – I thought about her to distraction.

I lavished attention on her when we were together. When we had sex – and it was often – I spent a lot of time on her erogenous spots, wanting to give her pleasure and make it good for her. I always made sure she came (although it was usually with my fingers or tongue).

Jen was my Goddess again. We'd lost that for a while. I'd lost that. But now she was my Goddess again. She was my everything. I loved her more than life.

I wished she wasn't so focused on *one* man. I wished she was open to bar hookups and one-night stands.

But she was only interested in Scott. I got it. I wanted a series of faceless fucks. She didn't want that. That wasn't her. And at the end of the day, it was her body. She got to choose.

Jen liked Scott a lot. They were good friends, buds. So not only did she get great sex, she also got to hang with a really good friend.

That's the part that made me the most concerned. That Jen might fall in love with Scott and leave me for him. As any cuck knows though, the risk of losing your wife to her lover is a big part of the fantasy. It's not something you want, but the risk is thrilling. Yes, it's fucked up. But the fantasy is what it is.

Then the routine changed. About 3 months after Stowe, Jen and I were in bed talking.

"Scott wants to move our dates to Saturday," she told me.

I frowned at that idea. "But you'll still go to your work's Friday happy hours? So you want to see him 2 nights a week now?"

"I'm not *with* Scott at the happy hours. He's just there," she replied. With a mischievous grin and a playful sparkle in her eyes, she added "Anyways, don't you want me to date my boyfriend more often?"

Calling Scott her "boyfriend" instead of her "lover" pushed my cuckold buttons. Calling their hookups "dates" did too. I'd told Jen that over countless pillow talks. I told her how it turned me on if she *dated* her *boyfriend* and really connected with him on an emotional level. It turned me on if her relationship with Scott was emotional in addition to physical.

Jen was all for that. Like I said, she didn't want faceless hookups. To her, one-night stands were slutty, and she didn't want to feel like a slut while playing our game. So it wasn't hard for me to convince her to think of Scott as her boyfriend and their time together as dates.

I also told Jen how this got me insanely jealous and insecure, and how I feared she'd leave me for him. Although the idea of losing her got me hot too. She always assured me I had nothing to worry about. They were friends – really good friends – but just friends.

"You know it's just fantasy. Of course, I don't want it to really happen," I said, referring to how the risk of losing her to Scott was part of my cuckold fantasies.

"Baby, don't worry, I get it. We all have fantasies that get us hot, that we don't want to really happen," Jen said, a reassuring smile on her face.

Jen was always smiling nowadays. She had an extra happy bounce in her step, and was always in a good mood. She was having a really fun time playing our game with Scott. Like, her work's happy hours were often more than drinking and goofing around singing karaoke. Sometimes her group of work friends (I called them the "Populars") went indoor golfing or rock climbing, or even bungee jumping. Jen was really athletic and social, and loved to be around her friends, so she was having a great time. Often, she told me it was like being in college again.

"So you want this? You want to change your date night to Saturdays?" I asked, already feeling the angst in the pit of my stomach.

"Well, yeah," she said with a helpless grin. She squeezed my hand reassuringly. "We're exploring things baby. That's what our game's about."

"And that means you want to spend more time with Scott," I said frowning at her, feeling jealous and worried. "It's not enough you already see him every day at work."

"It's not like that. Some days, alls we do is say hi as we pass in the hall," Jen said, giving me a playful pout to make the point she thought I was being a baby. "I can't exactly date Scotty if I don't see him more. Right?" She squeezed my cock over my boxers and found me hard. Grinning at me, she said "And I can see you like the idea of me seeing him more."

"Jen ... there's a difference between fantasy, and how I really feel," I told her.

"And you don't have anything to worry about," Jen assured me with another squeeze of my hand. "Me and Scotty are just buds. I'm *in like* with him and that's all it'll ever be. I'll never be *in love* with him like I am with you."

"It's just ... I like the whole weekend to reconnect with you," I said. I knew I must sound childish and pathetic to her, but I needed to tell her how I was feeling.

Jen hesitated, like she was deciding whether to tell me something. Then she hesitantly said, "That's part of why Scott wants to change to Saturdays."

"What?" I asked, not understanding.

"He wants to spend more time with me," Jen explained. "He says it's only fair, because I'm the only girl he's seeing."

"I didn't ask for that," I said immediately.

"I didn't either," Jen said. After a moment she added a little sheepishly, "But I admit it's flattering. And doesn't it make it feel more real?"

"Yes," I agreed as my heart began pounding in my chest. I was really hard now. Really hard.

Jen noticed. She pushed my boxers down. Then she wrapped her hand around my shaft and began to slowly stroke me.

"So that's why he wants to switch to Saturdays? To see you more?" I asked, breathing harder as she stroked me.

"Mostly I think," Jen said. She licked her hand for lubrication and then returned to stroking me. "But also, he wants us to feel like we're really dating. He says me going right back to being your wife ruins that."

"So Scott doesn't want you to reconnect with me," I said, breathing even harder.

"It's not about you baby," Jen said. "It's about me and Scotty."

I stared at her. Her words echoed in my head – "*It's about me and Scotty*." They weren't just fuck buddies. They really were a couple. A romantic, boyfriend-girlfriend couple. She was my wife, but she was also *in-like* with another man. I felt like I was about to cum.

"Wait," I said, grabbing her wrist. I didn't want to cum so fast.

"This really turns you on, huh?" she said giving me a lopsided grin.

"Yes," I admitted. "But I feel like he's taking you away from me. He's doing it on purpose."

"Mike, I'll be with you 5 nights a week. I'll only be with Scott 2 nights. That's not exactly taking me away from you."

I looked shocked at Jen. I couldn't believe how callous she was being about all of this. She saw my reaction and quickly said, "Okay, that didn't come out right. What I mean is, our game is like a hobby and we both really like it. It's not a lot to spend 2 nights a week on a hobby you really like. Right? And when I'm with Scott, it's not just me playing the game, it's both of us, because I know you'll be really hot the entire time. And I swear to you, Scotty and I are just buds. He'll never take me away from you."

"You promise to tell me if you start feeling like you're falling in love with him?" I said, reminding her of one of our rules. The most important rule. Along with being careful with birth control. Those were rules 1A and 1B.

"Of course, baby," she assured me. She was stroking me again. "God you're so hard," she said. I moved to get on top of her. I wanted to cum inside her. But she stopped me. She gently said, "Mike, remember, it's Wednesday."

I nodded, remembering. Jen wanted her pussy to look fresh for her dates with Scott, so that meant no intercourse after Tuesday. We started this a few weeks ago. When she suggested it, I was all for it as it really pushed my cuckold buttons. Now though it just added to my angst.

"But if we move your date night to Saturday, we can move Tuesday to Wednesday too," I said.

"Mike baby ... we just talked about this," Jen said gently. "Fridays will stay the same. So ...."

I didn't need her to finish the sentence. That meant she'd have sex with Scott on Friday *and* Saturday.

"This feels good though, right?" she asked as she continued to stroke me.

"Yeah," I said breathlessly. My head was swirling. I was in major cuck space, and incredibly aroused.

"Do you want to finish like this? Or in my mouth?" she asked.

"Your mouth," I said.

She smiled at me, and I rolled over onto my back. Then she pulled her long blonde hair back and took me into her mouth. Almost immediately I came.

Afterwards she got on her back and said, "Mike baby, can you ...?"

I nodded and moved down between her legs. I went down on her. Jen's libido had really picked up since we started playing the game, so she needed relief every night. I got her off at least once every day. Usually with my tongue. Jen loved my tongue. She's told me many times I'm the best she's ever had at oral.

As I licked her, I looked up into her face. Her eyes were closed and she was biting her lip, concentrating on reaching orgasm. God she looked so beautiful! She was probably fantasizing about Scott or maybe some other guy she found hot. I knew she wasn't fantasizing about me.

After cumming, Jen kissed me and snuggled into my arms. "I love you Mike," she said. "I love you so much."

I heard the sincerity in her voice and my heart leaped. I told her I loved her too. After a while, we got ready for bed. As usual, Jen put on my old frat t-shirt, VS cotton panties and white cotton ankle socks. She snuggled into me, and I spooned her, and we fell asleep that way.

CHAPTER 12

A couple days later, I was at the sports bar again, drinking beers with Scott. We were watching a summer league basketball game. He was boasting how his semi-pro team – the Bolts – could beat a bunch of summer and G-league teams. I doubted that but didn't bother arguing with him.

"I told you Jenny isn't the first married chick I've fucked. The guy I told you about, the dude who likes watching like you, he was my teammate last season," Scott said.

"You messed around with a teammate's wife?" I asked incredulously.

He shrugged as if conceding it wasn't the smartest move. "Yeah, it was dumb. It didn't end well and now he's on another team. Too bad, he could shoot the shit out of the ball. But what can I say? Married chicks are my weakness."

"Why?" I asked, incredibly intrigued.

"There's a reason they're married. The best looking girls get scooped up fast," Scott said. Then with a grin at me he added, "And it's fucking hot screwing another man's girl. There's nothing better than when she looks up at me with my dick stuffed in her, and we both know I'm fucking her better than her husband." His grin got even bigger as he said, "I see that look from your pretty wife all the time."

I glared at him. He shrugged and said, "Hate me if you want. Married pussy is easy to get into bed. Like Allie. Now she's got a sweet pussy."

"She was separated," I said.

"Yeah, I separated them," Scott joked with a laugh. Seeing my look of disgust, he laughed again and said, "Come on, I'm just joking. I met Allie's husband in Stowe. Seems like a good guy."

"RH is a good guy," I told him.

"Alright then, there you go," Scott said with a shrug. He abruptly pulled up his sleeve and pointed to an empty spot in his tattoo sleeve. "I'm getting a tat here Friday night," he said. "My buddy from Vegas, who inked most of my other tats, he's visiting some buddies here."

I nodded, not sure why he was telling me this. He grinned at me and said, "Jenny's got a sweet pussy too. Looks innocent, like a teenager's. Feels fucking incredible. Like a velvet glove around my cock."

I didn't say anything. I was suddenly breathing harder, but made an effort not to let Scott see. I wondered if he said these things to get to me.

"She's tight. Whew she's tight," Scott said with amazement in his voice. "Takes a while to get inside her. It's getting easier lately though. She's a slut, she wants every inch. Begs for it." He grinned at me and said, "Have you noticed Jenny's pussy getting looser?"

I didn't answer at once. I was trying to control my breathing. "Don't call my wife a slut," I finally said, my heart pounding in my chest. My dick was so hard it hurt.

"You know I don't mean anything by it," Scott said reasonably. "Jenny's one of my best friends. When it comes to sex though, she's a dirty slut. That's just who she is. It's like saying she has blonde hair. It's who she is."

"Whatever," I said under my breath.

"Jenny's a sweet girl," Scott continued, the grin still on his face. "Like her love tattoo. Honestly, I didn't notice it until she mentioned it. It's sweet. Just like her."

I didn't say anything. I was breathing hard though, and my heart pounded in my chest. I knew he was doing this on purpose. Pushing my cuckold buttons.

"I was surprised Jenny keeps a landing strip," Scott said. "Most hot chicks shave it all off, like porn stars. Here." He passed his iPhone to me.

"What?" I asked.

"Pictures of the chicks I've fucked recently," Scott said. He motioned to his phone. "Go ahead, look."

I stared at Scott for a moment. Then I thought, why not. I flipped through the pictures. I noticed a few things. All the girls were young and beautiful. All had completely bare pussies like the day they were born. Most had tats, more than Jen's single love tat. And most wore gold bands on their left hands – wedding rings.

I got to the pictures of Allie. I flipped through them slower, spending more time looking at them. Allie was truly beautiful and had an amazing body. While Jen was slim and petite, like an elegant ballerina, Allie was curvy and voluptuous, like a Playboy centerfold.

Allie had a few tats. They were all small and if you weren't looking, you might miss them. There was one on her ankle. Another on her lower back. One on her wrist. Tiny ones on each knee.

Scott noticed me spending more time looking at Allie's pictures. He grinned and said, "I get it. You've got the hots for Allie."

"No," I said immediately, maybe too quickly.

"You don't have to lie," Scott said with a laugh. "Look, I've got a thing for married girls. You want to fuck your wife's best friend. Don't worry, I won't tell Jenny. And Allie's hot. I don't blame you." With a laugh he added, "After all, I fucked her."

"You can tell Jen anything you want," I spat out. I wasn't going to keep secrets from Jen, just so Scott could use them against me later.

"And you can tell her anything I say too," he said with an unconcerned shrug.

I glared at Scott. Then I realized I hadn't gotten to his pictures of Jen. I quickly flipped through the pictures until I got to Jen. Many were nudes, while they were fucking. But a lot were of them hanging out together. I spent more time looking at those than the nudes. Many were selfies, others taken by a third person. They were kissing, leaning into each other, holding hands. Jen looked so into Scott. She looked like she was having fun, so happy to be with him.

Cuckold angst washed over me as I realized what the pictures were. They were pictures of a girlfriend with her boyfriend. And it was clear they were totally in-like with each other. Infatuated with each other.

"You're not posting them anywhere?" I said, my voice husky from excitement.

"No, of course not," Scott assured me. I believed him. For a guy who was able to get into the pants of so many hot girls, there was no need to post on the internet to brag about his conquests.

"I'm going to copy them," I told him, making it clear this wasn't a request. He shrugged like he didn't care. I used AirDrop to copy Jen's pictures to my iPhone.

Scott said, "Take the ones of Allie too." He smiled knowingly at me.

I admit I was tempted. But I didn't do it. Mostly because I'd be betraying RH. And also because then Scott would have something over me.

"So you won't go postal if Jen shaves off that landing strip, right?" Scott said, grinning at me. Seeing my scowl, he laughed and said, "Okay, sue me but I've got a thing for that barely legal look."

I didn't say anything. I was imaging Jen shaving her pussy for Scott. And I was remembering the pictures of Allie. Her pussy was shaved completely bare too.

CHAPTER 13

Friday night, Jen watched as the black tattoo artist – his name was Davis – worked on Scott's arm. She was fascinated by the intricate work. Davis was an artist, and Scott's beautiful body – in particular for this tat, his muscular forearm – was his canvas.

"It's so freaking awesome Scott," Jen gushed when Davis was done. Scott's arm was slightly red from the inking, but still she thought the skin-art was beautiful.

Davis gave Jen a toothy grin. He was a big man, bigger even than Scott, and wore his long jet-black hair in corn rolls. Even though he was smiling, he looked kind of dangerous. Jen wasn't racist, but the way the tattoo artist towered over her with his ripped muscular body and jet-black skin intimidated her.

"You inked?" Davis asked.

"She's got one," Scott said, answering for Jen. "Show him Jenny."

Jen had done a couple shots of vodka along with Scott before Davis worked on him, so she was feeling tipsy. Also, she kinda liked the idea of showing her body to the dangerous looking black man. So Jen unzipped her skinny jeans and pushed them down enough to show Davis her tat on her hip.

Davis ran his finger along the black line work. His hands were calloused. "Nice work," he said. "Love right?" When Jen nodded, he said "Small though." The Japanese love symbol was barely a half inch across.

"I like the way Kate Moss does it," Jen said. "She has tats but they're all really small. My girlfriend Allie does it that way too."

"Lucian Freud inked Kate's back tats," Davis said. "Cost a million bucks."

"I guess I won't be getting Lucian to ink me then," Jen said with a laugh.

"He died," Davis said with an indulgent smile.

"Oh sorry," Jen said. She tried to pull up her jeans, but Davis curled a finger in the waist and stopped her.

"I'll ink you," Davis offered. "No charge."

"Don't listen to his bullshit Jenny," Scott said, leaning against the table and grinning. "Davis always charges something."

Davis grinned at Scott, then looked back at Jen. He slid his curled finger from Jen's hip to above her pussy. He moved his finger back and forth across her tiny, trimmed landing strip. "I'm sure we can work something out," he said grinning at her.

Jen felt really naughty, and it wasn't just the vodka. God she'd changed so much. Not too long ago she'd been a faithful, prim and proper wife. Now she was having a wild affair with Scott. She'd cheated with her husband's 18-year-old friend. And she was in a tattoo parlor in a bad part of Harlem getting almost fingered by a big black man. Jen had never felt so alive, or had so much fun!

Jen hooked her thumbs in her pants and pushed them down another inch. Now her tiny landing strip was in view. "You think so?" she asked Davis in a low throaty voice.

"Oh yes indeed," Davis said, his eyes locked on Jen's sexy flat tummy and trimmed blonde bush. "Pretty white girls like you, we can always work something out."

Scott laughed and put his arm around Jen, pulling her away from Davis. "Davis, stay the fuck away from my girl," he said with a laugh. "Jenny you slut, pull up your pants," he said with another good-natured laugh.

Jen laughed too as she pulled up her skinny jeans. She smiled at Davis, and he smiled back at her.

Later they were at Scott's apartment. Both were sweating and panting after fantastic sex. "I better go," Jen said looking at the clock. She promised Mike she'd be home by midnight. It was Friday and her official date night with Scott was tomorrow— their first Saturday night date—so she didn't want to push it.

"Wait, you've got time," Scott said, pulling her back to him. He ran his finger underneath her breast. "This is where you should get inked," he said.

"I'm not going to get a tattoo on my breast Scott," Jen said with a frown.

"Not *on* your breast. I would never want to mar perfect," he said with a grin at her. "I'm talking *under* your breast." Again, he ran his fingertip along the soft skin just below the curve of her small, perky A-cup breast. "Maybe tiny lettering, or a vine, or numbers. It's really hot."

Jen considered it. Then she shook her head and said, "Mike would hate it. I told you. He hates tats."

"You're thinking about getting inked by Davis, I can tell," he said knowingly.

"Yeah, but not on my breast, or close to it," Jen said. "Mike would hate it."

"He might hate it, but it'll make his dick hard," Scott said with a laugh. "He practically had a heart attack when I showed him the pictures of you. Of us."

Jen smiled. She thought Mike would insist Scott delete them, but all he did was copy them to his phone. The more they played the game, the more she learned about her husband.

"He drooled over Allie's pictures," Scott said, grinning at her.

"Every man drools over Allie," Jen said with a shrug.

"I think Mike seriously wants to get inside Allie's pants," Scott said, the grin still on his face.

"If you're trying to make me jealous you can stop," Jen snapped. "Mike would never cheat on me. And he respects Allie and RH too much."

"Okay, whatever," Scott said with a shrug. He watched Jen get dressed. As she pulled on her thong he said, "Do something for me. To celebrate our first Saturday night date."

"What?" she asked.

"Shave off your bush," Scott said.

"You don't think it's sexy?" Jen asked, looking down at her landing strip.

"I like it better completely bare," Scott said.

Jen didn't say yes, but she didn't say no, as she finished dressing.

Scott said, "So you're going back to Mike, your roommate?" He said it as a question, but it was a statement too.

"Yeah, right, my roommate," Jen said with a laugh.

"We've got a date tomorrow, so until then Mike is your roommate," Scott said with a grin.

"Okay, whatever," Jen said with another laugh.

Scott pulled Jen to him. "So you treat Mike like your roommate until after our date tomorrow," he said, still grinning at her. "Your platonic roommate."

"Huh," Jen said as she realized what Scott was saying. And the implications. She grinned at him and said, "You're enjoying this aren't you?"

"I'm having a shitload of fun," Scott said with a grin back.

———◉———

Like every Friday, I paced the floor waiting for Jen to get home. This time though, not only did I have to deal with tonight, I had to deal with tomorrow night too. This was my new reality. Scott got my wife 2 nights a week. I got her 5. I got more than twice the nights. But mine were the work nights. He got the best nights, Friday and Saturday, the weekend nights.

I avoided drinking and beating off. I didn't want the depression that came after. I tried to focus on work. We were close to going live with Sapphire. I hoped to make enough money in bonuses to buy Jen a real house. Maybe then we'd stop playing the game. Jen would go off the pill, and we'd start a family. Although to be honest, despite all the angst, I wasn't ready for that yet. Life was too exciting right now. My dick was constantly hard. I wanted to experience this lifestyle a while longer, and I knew Jen did too.

Finally, the door opened and Jen was there. I immediately pulled her into my arms. I tried to kiss her but she turned her head so I got her cheek instead of her lips. "Wait Mike we have to talk," she said pulling away from me.

"What?" I asked, even more agitated now.

We sat on the sofa. Jen said, "Scott thinks I should treat you like my roommate, until after our date tomorrow."

"What?" I said, frowning.

"He has a point Mike," she said. "It'll feel more real if I'm Scott's girlfriend all the way from Friday to Saturday.

"What about reconnecting?" I said.

"We're still together all day tomorrow until my date," Jen said. "We're still best friends. Soul mates."

"But what does it mean, roommates?" I asked, trying to understand this new twist in the game.

"It means best friends," Jen said. "Platonic friends. We'll talk. I'll tell you all about Scott. What we did tonight. You're my best friend. I'll tell you everything."

"But we're *platonic* friends?" I said dumbly, trying to catch up to the concept.

"This way, from Friday night to Sunday morning, I'll feel like Scott's my boyfriend," Jen said. "You'll feel that way too. It'll feel real to us. So we both get to explore our fantasies."

"But I can't touch you?" I said.

"No. Or see me," Jen added.

"I can't see you?" I said incredulously.

"No, Mike," Jen said with a frown, frustrated I was taking so long to understand this simple concept. "We're platonic friends."

"What about sleeping together?" I said with a frown. There had to be limits to this game. Jen realized it too because she said, "Well, when I sleep over with Allie we usually sleep in the same bed, so I guess that's okay. But I'll wear PJs. And you can't touch me." Normally to bed I wore boxers, and she wore my frat t-shirt that covered her butt but left her legs completely exposed. She was saying I wouldn't see any skin except her hands, feet and head.

"This is fucked up Jen," I told her.

"No, it's fun," Jen said with a grin, and she playfully poked me in the arm. "You're having fun. I can tell," she said looking at the erection in my pants. Seeing the distressed look on my face, she got serious and admitted, "I know right now I'm really crushing on Scotty. I just want to experience it. The romance and all."

I felt like my heart was breaking. "It's hard hearing you say that," I said.

"Mike baby, I know the difference between a crush and love. I'm in-like with Scott but that's all. Eventually the infatuation will go away, and we'll go back to being just buds again. You know, without the benefits part. And anyways, you want this too. You've told me that. You want my relationship with Scott to be physical *and* emotional."

"Then what about us?" I asked.

"Baby, nothing between us has changed," she assured me. "My feelings for you are 100% the same." She squeezed my hand reassuringly and said, "Okay?"

I hesitated, then nodded my head and said, "Okay."

Jen looked at me, as if studying me. Then she said, "I'm going to do something. I'm telling you because you're my best friend. I want to make sure you can handle it."

"What?"

"You won't know until I do it," she said.

"How can I know if I can handle it if I don't know what it is?" I said.

"Because you're my best friend and that's what best friends do. They trust each other. They handle things," Jen said, a playful impish smile on her face.

It was that impish smile on her beautiful face that decided it for me. I couldn't help giving her a grin back. "Okay, I'll handle it. What?"

Jen grinned at me. "I'll be right back," she said, and she went into the bathroom. I heard the water running. A few minutes later she rejoined me on the sofa.

"What?" I asked.

"I think you know," Jen said, that playful smile still on her face. "Scotty said you talked about it."

I did know too. "You shaved it off," I said, my stomach churning.

"Yes," she said.

"For Scott."

"Yes," she admitted. "I shave it off for Scott. He said he wanted me completely bare."

We were looking at each other. I knew we were thinking the same thing. When we first met, Jen used to keep herself completely bare. One time though – we had just become exclusive to each other – I jokingly said maybe she wasn't a natural blonde. So since then, for almost 10 years, Jen has kept a little trimmed landing strip, to prove to me she was a natural blonde. It was a little inside joke, the kind all married couples have. It was something Jen did for me because I was her husband, and she loved me.

Now with a couple swipes of a razor, it was gone. What Jen used to do for me, she now did for Scott. And I couldn't even see it. I wasn't allowed. Not until after their date tomorrow. The feelings of jealousy, hurt, and denial were overwhelming. But god I was so hard. My heart was beating so wildly, it was sending so much blood to my dick it hurt.

"If I touch myself I'll cum," I admitted.

"I thought so," Jen said. With the playful smile still on her pretty face, she added "But I don't think that's an appropriate thing to say to your platonic best friend."

I was seriously having a hard time breathing.

"Since I've got your attention, I want to tell you something else," she said.

"Okay, I'll try to handle it," I said with a laugh.

Jen laughed with me. Then she said, "I'm going to get another tattoo. Don't worry. It'll be really small like my other one."

I stared at her, shocked. "So I have no say in this?" I said bitterly. "You're getting a tattoo for Scott and I have no say in it?"

"I'm getting the tattoo for *me*," Jen said. "Scotty's encouraging me, but it's for me."

"That's bullshit Jen!" I said angrily at her.

Jen paused as if counting to 10, allowing me to calm down. Then she said, "Mike baby, you know why I'm having so much fun with Scott? Because I have you. I know he's an ass. I like him but he's an ass. But I can let myself go and have fun with him because I know I have you. I love you more now than ever baby, because you're letting me be me. Don't you like this me? Don't you like JenJen's back?"

"I love this you," I said begrudgingly. "It's just … I feel like I have no control."

"Just go with it Mike," Jen implored me. "Trust me. We won't play the game forever."

"And when we stop playing, you'll be just mine again right?"

"Yes," Jen assured me, smiling into my eyes. "I'll be your prim and proper, faithful wife again."

"That doesn't sound too exciting," I joked.

"Well ...," Jen said with a resigned shrug, and we both laughed. "We better go to bed. I have a date with Scotty tomorrow and I need my beauty sleep." She looked at the tent in my pants and, with a smile, added "But maybe you better take a cold shower before getting into bed with me."

CHAPTER 14

The next day, Jen's date was to go watch Scott and his basketball team – the Bolts – play their next game. She invited me to go along because she knew I liked watching sports. And she also knew I liked watching her with Scott. Not just the sex part, but her acting like his girlfriend. It caused me a lot of angst, but that was a big part of the fantasy for me.

Jen wore 4-inch Christian Louboutin high heels – the ones with the sexy red bottoms—with her skinny jeans, so she was really dressed to impressed. I think she was nervous to meet Scott's basketball friends (and their wives and girlfriends) for the first time. On top she wore a long sleeve blouse. Even though it was loose, the blouse draped perfectly over and around her breasts. It was clear she was braless, and that surprised me. Or maybe it didn't, because I knew Scott liked her braless and it was clear my wife's goal was to look as fuckable as possible for him. The top had long sleeves that went to her palms. I always thought that was cute, and it was something she wore all the time.

Jen was still modest enough to wear a jacket on top, and I saw her constantly tugging it closed to cover the dents made by her nipples.

Before the game, Scott introduced Jen to his friends as his new girlfriend. I can't tell you the charge I got out of that. Especially the way Jen squeezed Scott's hand and smiled into his eyes as he introduced her around.

Scott introduced me as one of Jen's friends from college. Which was true of course. I thought it was smart. Always lie with the truth. I thought it was ironic too; now it was me who was Jen's "best bud."

I sat next to Jen during the game. Not too close of course, and no holding hands or even leaning into each other. In fact, I hadn't touched my wife in any kind of intimate way since her date with Scott last night. Jen hugged me last night when we went to bed, but she pulled away when I tried to spoon her. It'd been a very long, frustrating evening (and I was so excited I ended up masturbating twice while Jen slept beside me).

Jen chatted with the other wives and girlfriends as she watched Scott play. I have to admit, he was good. Jen's not a big basketball fan, but even she could see his talent. I could tell she was impressed. Or maybe she just enjoyed watching Scott's athletic body moving up and down the court.

"Scotty says he plays power guard," Jen said to me at one point.

"You mean power forward," I said. "There's no such thing as power guard."

"I don't know ...," Jen said hesitantly. "I'm sure he said power guard."

"Jen he's making it up. There's no such thing as power guard," I said, exasperation leaking into my voice.

"I'm sure Scotty said power *guard,* Mike," Jen insisted.

I hated when she called him Scotty. I hated it.

"Do you always have to take his side?" I whispered.

Jen rolled her eyes at me. She rolled her eyes! At me!

Just then, we watched Scott violently swat away a layup and then race down court. He posted up against the opposing center, pivoted and then slammed down a dunk. Jen pointed at the court and said, "I mean Mike. The way Scotty plays. Doesn't power guard fit him?"

At that moment, I knew what it felt like to be completely emasculated.

After the game, the team went to a bar to celebrate their victory. Jen was attached to Scott. I drifted off and chatted with some of his friends. The wives and girlfriends were extremely interested in Jen as she was the "*new girl*" in the group.

They talked me up to try to get the 411. "Why does Jen wear a wedding ring?" one wife asked me. "Is she married?"

I sputtered, not knowing what to say. I cursed our lack of planning. Why didn't we talk about this ahead of time? I didn't want to say she was cheating on her husband, as I didn't want them to lose respect for her. So I sputtered out, "Jen and her husband are separated."

"Oh," the wife said. All the other wives and girlfriends were closely listening. "Are they splitting for good? Because Jen looks really into Scott. And he looks really into her."

"I don't know," I said, looking over at Jen. She *did* look really into Scott. And really happy to be with him.

I got a private moment with Jen and I told her what happened. "Oh god Mike. Why didn't you say I wear it so I don't get hit on?" she whispered with alarm in her voice.

"I didn't think of that," I said apologetically. Fuck! Why didn't I think of that?!

"It would have been so much easier if they thought I was single," Jen lamented. "I should've left the rings at home."

I looked at her in shock. "Those rings are your wedding and engagement rings!" I reminded her. "Remember? You and me? We're married? This is supposed to be just a game. And our rule is you don't take the rings off."

"Okay, okay," Jen said, conceding the point. But I could tell she wasn't happy about it.

"Fine Jen whatever," I hissed, angrily stomping away from her.

"Wait, stop," she whispered grabbing my wrist. "I'm sorry. I'm nervous being around his friends. I feel like everyone's judging me. It's like back in high school."

Her vulnerability softened me. "Just say you're separated," I told her. "You don't have to get into the details."

"You're sure you're okay with that?"

I wasn't sure. But I forced a smile and said, "Yeah. It's just a game, right?"

Jen smiled at me, looking relieved. "Scotty's really excited to see what I did last night," she said with an excited sparkle in her eyes.

I knew she was talking about how she shaved off her landing strip. I felt my already hard cock jerk in my pants. "You tell him you're getting another tattoo?" I asked.

"Yes. He can't stop talking about it," she said excitedly. Despite what she said last night, I felt like she was getting inked *for Scott*. It really upset me. She was *my* wife and her body was supposed to be mine. But she was going to permanently mark her body for another man.

Jen read my mind. "I'm getting it for *me* Mike. I'm not doing it for Scott," she assured me. "I shaved my landing strip for Scott, but I can grow that back. You get the difference, right?"

I nodded. Even though she was trying to soothe my feelings, I noticed how she wasn't giving me any say in the matter. Who was this woman? She'd changed so much in just a few months. But then I knew. This was the feisty and flirty, "most popular girl on campus" Jenny Johnson I first met in college. Despite how much it was churning my stomach, I was happy to have this JenJen back.

After the bar we rode an uber to our apartment. I rode in front while Jen rode with Scott in the back. The 3 of us talked, but like always, it was mostly Jen and Scott talking and laughing with me barely getting a word in. They were the couple, and I was the third wheel friend.

Once we got to our apartment building, we realigned somewhat. We obviously couldn't risk our neighbors seeing Jen hanging on to another man's hand. So Jen took my hand for the short journey to our apartment. But Scott walked next to her, so close their bodies almost touched.

As soon as we got in our apartment, Jen squeezed my hand, then she went back to being Scott's girlfriend. I went to make drinks and when I got back, I found them making out on the sofa. Then they moved to our bedroom.

When I joined them, Scott was leaning against the wall, and Jen was on her knees with his dick in her mouth. He looked at me with lust-filled eyes and breathlessly said, "Your wife gives good head."

We'd agreed ahead of time Scott would spend the night. With Jen. So I slept in the bedroom we'd converted from a small den (the room Joey used to sleep in). I watched them fuck for a while but frankly I couldn't watch too long. It got me too worked up, both sexually and emotionally. I hadn't touched Jen intimately in over 24 hours and I was going out of my mind. It wasn't just I wanted her sexually, but I needed to reconnect with her.

I tossed and turned all night. A couple times I went to the bedroom. The first time they were fucking, the room lit only by moonlight. Scott was on top of Jen, and he was long stroking her really slow. As they fucked, they kissed and looked into the other's eyes. They were making love really, not fucking. The sight broke my heart but got me so hard. I slowly stroked myself, my hand moving at the same pace as their love making. When I came the depression hit and I staggered back to the guest bed.

The second time they were asleep. Normally when we sleep, Jen sleeps on her side and I spoon her from behind. But now, Scott was on his back with his arm around Jen. She was snuggled into his chest, her arm draped over his chest, her long shapely leg over his. They looked so much like a couple, sleeping with their bodies tangled that way. I got my phone and took pictures of them. Then I went back to the guest bed and masturbated as I flipped back and forth through the pictures.

When I woke up, the sun was up. Jen was gently shaking my shoulder. "Come to bed baby," she softly said to me.

Scott was gone. Jen had showered and remade the bed. She was wearing my frat t-shirt. She was my wife again.

We made love with me on top. I moved in and out slow. I needed to reconnect with her more than I needed an orgasm, and she was sore and satiated after spending all night impaled on Scott's dick.

Jen's pussy felt really loose, and that inflamed me. But I'd masturbated so much the day before I was able to last.

"I'm sorry I was such a bitch to you last night, at the game," she told me. "I was nervous. It's like high school and college. Scott's friends are the popular clique and I'm the new girl. They're nice but standoffish. They don't want to get to know me because they think Scott'll have another girl at the next game."

"Does that make you jealous?" I asked.

Jen hesitated, then said, "Is it terrible if I say yes? I mean, I know it's just a game. It's not real. But I can't help feeling what I'm feeling."

With a lump in my throat, I asked, "Do you love him, Jen?"

"I don't love him," Jen replied. "I'm crushing on him, but I don't love him."

"How can you tell, if you're that into him?" I asked. "His friends, those girls, they said you look so into him. You *do* look into him."

"Well, hopefully he's into me too," Jen said.

"Of course he is, but it's you I care about," I said.

Jen thought about it, as if trying to find the right words to explain how she was feeling. "I can feel love for Scotty, but not love him," she said. "Does that make sense?"

"So you *do* love him," I said with a heavy heart.

"Mike baby, did you hear what I just said? *Feeling* love is not the same as *being in love*. It's not."

"It's just ... I don't know where this is headed," I said. "I mean look at us. I'm not allowed inside you after Tuesday. I can't touch you or even see your body Friday or Saturday. He's wedging himself between us." I hesitated, then said, "I'm close to vetoing things, Jen."

It was our rule. If either of us wanted to end the game, we could end it. We both had veto power.

Jen frowned at me. "I'd be really unhappy if you did that," she told me. "We've started on a journey Mike. You pushed me into this. And now I feel the way I feel. You can't just end it like that. I'll be really upset if you did."

I stopped moving inside her. I looked at her and said, "What are you saying? You'd pick Scott over me?" I felt dread, not wanting to hear her answer, but I had to know.

"I'm saying what I just said," Jen said stubbornly. "I'd be really unhappy. I'd be mad at you, and resentful too."

I stared at her. "So you *are* picking Scott over me?" I asked incredulously. I bitterly added, "Ten years means nothing to you?"

Jen frowned at me. Then she moved me onto my back. She straddled my hips and guided my cock back into her. She rocked back and forth on my shaft. "You know I've never felt you so hard," she said looking into my eyes.

"Don't change the subject," I said angrily.

"This *is* the subject Mike," Jen said reasonably. "I read all those stories you showed me. I still read Literotica and ourhotwives sometimes. You love this. Don't lie, you do. Me crushing on Scott. Dressing special for him. Wanting him inside me. Even falling in love with him. That's what you want Mike. It pushes all your cuckold buttons. Remember? I said sometimes it might feel like you're losing me to Scott. Not that you *are* losing me. But it might *feel* that way. And you said you wanted that."

"What are you saying?" I said, breathing hard and my heart pounding.

"I'm saying you need to trust me," Jen said as she continued to rock back and forth on my cock. She wrapped her arms around my neck and kissed me. "You need to let things play out. I'm in-like with Scott. That's all. Not love. Like. You need to trust me."

I hesitated, then said, "I do trust you. It's just hard sometimes. Like last night, when I couldn't touch you."

"I felt you masturbating," she said with a grin at me.

"Twice actually," I said with a sheepish grin back.

Jen giggled. "See? You get off on it. It was hard for me too last night. But when I woke up this morning, I still felt like Scott's girlfriend. That's our game. It pushes both our buttons."

I knew she was right. And it was all easier to deal with, holding her in my arms, with my dick inside her.

"Can I tell you something?" Jen said.

"Yes," I replied.

"Scott's been pushing me to stop using condoms," she said. "He took a test. He's clean. He swears he's only seeing me and I believe him."

I stared at my wife, processing this information. "Do you want this?" I asked.

"Yes," Jen said without any hesitation. With a sheepish smile, she added, "Skin-to-skin always feels better right?"

I knew it was more than physical pleasure. Skin-to-skin was more intimate, and Jen was really crushing on Scott. Scott was crushing on her too. They wanted that intimate physical connection.

"You'll let him cum inside you?" I asked, my heart beating wildly.

"Yes, I'll let him," Jen said. "I want him to cum inside me."

I stared at her. Then my body lurched, and I came.

CHAPTER 15

Of course, I agreed. I mean, it wasn't like Jen was giving me a choice. It was more like she was just telling me what she was going to do anyway. Also, I knew things had been heading towards this. And truthfully, I wanted it as much as Jen. I wanted Scott bare inside her. I wanted their fluids and hormones to mix. I wanted them to grow even closer.

Yes it was fucked up. I was fucked up. But I couldn't help how I felt.

I thought a lot about what Jen said. She might *feel* love for Scott, but not be *in love* with him. That's what I wanted. I wanted her to feel love for him. I knew it was a dangerous game. How close was "feeling love" to "being in love"? But now I was obsessed with the game. I wanted to do more. I wanted to push the boundaries.

We added 2 more rules to our game. First, Jen had to be super careful about taking the pill. That had already been an unstated rule, but now obviously it was absolutely critical she too the birth control pill everyday. Second, Jen could let Scott bare inside her only when she wasn't ovulating. Otherwise he had to wear condoms. Because the pill wasn't foolproof.

Jen had been good about Rule #1. As for Rule #2, we checked the calendar and she wasn't ovulating this weekend. So this weekend it was. Jen would let Scott inside her without a condom. And she would let him cum inside her. Once we decided this, I got so excited my body shook uncontrollably.

We made love Monday and Tuesday. Gently because Jen was sore from Scott. But then, as usual, Jen cut me off Wednesday morning. She wanted her pussy to look fresh for Scott. She wouldn't even let me go down on her. She wanted to be extra horny for Scott on Friday night.

Then Friday morning, a wrench got thrown into the works. It was a good thing though. My bosses at work decided to launch Sapphire early. We'd recently fixed some thorny bugs and the powers-that-be decided it was time.

It was a very big day for me, by far the biggest of my professional career. Everyone from file clerks to even old man Jacob himself congratulated me. The number crunchers and partners in San Francisco, Chicago and London called me or emailed me with congrats. In my office, I opened a bottle of champagne with my team and we toasted ourselves.

I called Jen. I obviously wanted to celebrate with her, so it meant she had to nix her evening's plans with Scott. After all, the game was just a game. The launch of Sapphire was real life.

Jen was really happy for me. I heard disappointment in her voice since she'd been excited to see Scott, but she definitely wanted to celebrate with me instead. The fact she immediately agreed to cancel her plans with Scott to celebrate with me made me feel really good.

Then around 5pm, Jen called me. "You won't believe this! Scott just got promoted to full partner!" she said sounding awestruck.

"Already?" I asked. I was shocked myself. Before, Scott had been a *junior* partner. It usually took 4 or 5 years to make the jump to *full* partner. Scott had done it in just over a year.

"Yeah, it's freaking amazing!" she said excitedly.

"It doesn't seem fair. You were team lead on Kelloggs," I said. Jen had recently landed her first big account, the Kellogg company. If they were going to advance someone so quickly, why not my wife rather than Scott?

"It's okay. I'm really happy for him. I couldn't have done Kelloggs without him," she gushed. I would rather she not be so enthused about his promotion, but didn't say anything knowing it was petty.

Then she said, "A lot of people are going out tonight to celebrate." She hesitantly added, "I should probably make an appearance."

"Okay," I said warily. My spider-sense was tingling but I'd be a jerk to say no.

Jen sounded appreciative for my understanding. "Can you stop by the bar?" she asked. "We'll leave from there."

Scott was the center of attention of course. Jen was next to him, smiling and looking really happy for him. I stood beside her and listened as Scott held court.

I'd been there about 10 minutes before Jen seemed to remember and said, "Oh baby, congrats about Sapphire!" She hugged and kissed me, although her praise felt bittersweet since she seemed more impressed with Scott's promotion than my Sapphire launch.

I told Jen we needed to bolt to make our reservation. Scott heard me and insisted we go out with them, to celebrate both our big days. I didn't want to, but I could tell Jen did, so I reluctantly agreed.

At dinner, the talk was mostly gossip about work. On top of that I barely knew anyone. I felt like a complete third wheel.

At one point, Jen announced to everyone my Sapphire project had launched. "Oh yeah, how's that going bro?" Scott said.

There wasn't a lot I could say. I mean, Sapphire wasn't something sexy like a big high-tech IPO. Sapphire worked in the background, slowly at first and gaining steam over time. Our analytics predicted tangible results in 2-3 months. When you're talking about a radical change to how people would invest in the stock market, 2-3 months wasn't a big deal. But it wasn't an interesting story, especially to non-technical marketing types at a trendy New York City Italian-French fusion restaurant.

On top of that, I was uncomfortable being the center of attention. And I was a terrible pubic speaker. So I stumbled over my answer to Scott's question. Everyone gave me a half-hearted toast, and then their attention quickly returned to office gossip and Scott's promotion. Jen squeezed my hand and whispered, "I'm really proud of you." But she quickly returned to talking to her co-workers, focusing a lot of her attention again on Scott.

I went to the bathroom. Mostly just to get some air. Passing the bar, I glanced at the TV. Anderson Cooper on CNN was doing a short blurb on this new investment vehicle called Sapphire. I asked the bartender to switch to Fox. Coincidentally, Jasmine Kelly was talking about Sapphire too. Jasmine used to be a sideline reporter for ESPN, like Erin Andrews. In fact, she looked like a younger Ein Andrews (Jasmine was about a decade younger than Erin). She'd recently jumped to Fox to be one of their news anchors. I followed some of the news blogs and everyone agreed Jasmine was a rising star in the new business.

I stayed and watched for a while. It made me feel better to hear Sapphire – *my* Sapphire – being discussed on these big-time news channels. No one on CNN or Fox would be talking about Scott's stupid promotion.

When I got back, people were starting to leave. Jen and Scott weren't there. "Where's Jen?" I asked Allie.

"She went outside for a smoke," Allie said. Jen was a social smoker, especially at gatherings like this.

"With Scott?" I asked with a frown.

Allie didn't answer. Instead, she said "Sit here Mike and tell me about Sapphire."

I narrowed my eyes suspiciously at her. Allie was not the kind of person to be interested in Sapphire. She might be great at marketing but math and computers were not her thing. I made a beeline for the door, with Allie yelling behind me, "Mike, wait."

Scott and Jen weren't outside. Then I remembered this restaurant had a downstairs banquet room for parties. I went downstairs and looked inside. The room was dark but light from streetlamps let me see everything.

Scott was leaning against a table. Jen was on her knees with his dick in her mouth. "That's it. Suck it," he hissed to her. "You love this cock, don't you?"

Even with her mouth stuffed with his cock, she was able to say, "Cum fast Scott. I have to get back."

"Suck me better and I'll cum faster," he joked with a chuckle. I saw Jen smile.

"Please Scott, cum fast, Mike's waiting," she pleaded. She was using her hands on him too now. One hand on top of the other, stroking his shaft in rhythm with her head bobbing back and forth. His cock was so long, thick and heavy, she couldn't hold him all even with both hands.

"I love hearing you beg," Scott said with a grin. He gripped her head with his hands, curling his fingers into her long blonde hair. "I'm your boss now. This is your place. On your knees sucking my dick."

I heard Jen moan. I could tell she was in major sub-space.

I couldn't take anymore. I went back upstairs. Everyone was gone except for Allie. She could see it in my face. She knew I saw them.

"Jen loves you," Allie told me consolingly. "She's just going through something right now."

I nodded, barely hearing her. I asked, "How's RH?"

Allie hesitated. "He's ... not here," she said.

I looked at her. I saw she was sad. "I'm sorry," I said. She shrugged.

Then she hesitantly asked, "Jen says ... you're into this?"

It didn't surprise me. Allie was Jen's best friend, they talked about everything. So of course Jen told Allie about our game and my fantasies. "So this is where you tell me I'm pathetic, right?" I said bitterly.

"I don't think you're pathetic Mike," Allie said. "I'm just surprised, that's all." Now it was my turn to shrug. She studied me, then said "If it makes you so unhappy, why do it?"

I laughed. It was one of those *I have no fucking clue* laughs.

"You don't have to worry. Jen really loves you," she assured me.

"She talks about me?" I asked.

"She talks about you a lot Mike," Allie replied.

"She talks about Scott a lot too though, right?"

Allie shrugged, as if saying "*why ask if you know the answer?*"

"I better go," she said, getting up.

"Thanks for talking to me," I said. I meant it too.

"You know I think this is the most we've ever talked," she said grinning at me.

"I think you're right," I said with a grin back.

"Well, congrats on Sapphire, whatever it is," she joked, still grinning at me. Then she was gone.

I moved to the bar and ordered a scotch. They didn't have Highland Park so I got a Macallan. I like scotch but I'm not an expert. They all mostly taste the same to me. To be honest, I usually drink Highland Park because I think it's a cool name.

Sometime later, I saw Jen rush up from downstairs, with Scott right behind her. She looked alarmed seeing our table empty. Then she saw me. She whispered something to Scott. He nodded. I saw them squeeze hands briefly, then Scott left. The image of them squeezing hands got burned in my brain, as much as the sight downstairs of Jen with Scott's cock in her mouth.

Jen came over to me and sat beside me. "I'm sorry," she whispered to me. Jen had put herself back together, so she didn't look like a girl who had just been on her knees giving a blowjob. But I could smell cum on her breath.

I said bitterly, "I guess you don't mind cum breath when you're with me."

Jen stared at me and was quiet, like she was counting to 10. Then she took my scotch and took a long sip, swirling the golden liquid in her mouth. After she swallowed, she said again "I'm sorry."

When I didn't respond, she said pleadingly, "Mike will you say something?"

I paused, counting to 10 myself. Then I hissed in a low voice, "I'm just trying to imagine the circumstances that led you downstairs to give Scott a blowjob. On this day of all days."

Jen winced at my sarcastic rebuke. In a soft voice, she said "We went outside for a smoke. One thing led to another. I don't know ...."

"You don't *know*?!" I spat out incredulously.

"I know you're really mad, and you have every right to be," Jen said. "But it's not easy. I have you *and* Scott. I have to keep both of you happy."

"I'm your husband!" I reminded her.

"Of course you are Mike. But he's supposed to be my boyfriend, right? He thought we were getting together tonight. He has needs just like you. I have to take care of him, just like I have to take care of you."

"You're *my* girl!" I said. "He can get his own girl!"

"Mike come on ...," she said pleadingly. I knew she was right. We were playing a game, and in this game – in my new reality – Jen was Scott's girl too.

"You could be more discreet about it!" I said angrily.

"I know. We were absolutely wrong," Jen said, surrendering completely. "People were leaving. No one noticed. It just happened. But we were wrong. I'm really sorry Mike."

My stomach was churning big time. I hated the way she used "*we*" to refer to her and Scott. "We" used to be us.

"You're such a good guy about tonight," Jen said, squeezing my hand.

"Jen – just stop, okay?" I said irritably. "You're not making it better. I'm mad. And I just have to be mad until I'm not mad anymore."

"But you *are* a great guy. You were willing to share your special day. Scott would never do that. He's too selfish. I know that. That's why I love you, Mike."

"But you let him do this to you," I said, running my thumb over her knees. Her stockings were scuffed from being on her knees for Scott.

Jen gave me a helpless shrug, as if saying "*I love you but I can't resist Scott*."

"I saw you sucking him off," I said. "He said he's your boss now. What's that mean?"

"The partners did a reorg," Jen explained. "Scott's in charge of Kelloggs so now I work for him. So does Allie. He's our boss now."

"*You* got Kelloggs!" I protested. "It's *your* project!"

"It's okay Mike. I don't mind," Jen said soothingly, rubbing my arm to calm me. "I don't know what I'm doing half the time, and Scott's got way more experience. He's really smart and talented. I can learn a lot working for him." With a grin she added, "All day he teased me. How now I work for him. So now I have to do anything he wants."

"That doesn't make you mad?"

"Mike baby he's joking," Jen said. "It's actually hot. You must know by now I get off on that. You know I'm a bottom. And Scotty's my top."

I was quiet, processing that. Yes, I did already know that. But it still hurt to hear her say it.

I said, "I've never been your top, have I?"

To her credit, she didn't lie. She rubbed my arm and said, "It's not your personality. If that was really important to me, I wouldn't have married you. But I *did* marry you. So that proves it's not that important to you."

"Except you get off on being Scott's bottom," I said.

"It's just the game, Mike," Jen said squeezing my hand again. "And I think – *I know* – you get off on it too."

Holding my hand, Jen said, "You know what I've figured out? And don't take this the wrong way. It doesn't affect at all my feelings for you. But I think you're kinda a bottom too. Right? You saw me going down on Scott. You were mad but didn't do anything. Just like when you saw Scott figuring me at Stowe. It gets you more turned on than upset. And that's okay. That's your fantasy, and it's okay. That's why we're playing the game."

I was quiet again, trying to come to grips with what Jen was saying. Finally I said, "If I'm a bottom, who's my top?"

"Don't worry, it's not Scott," Jen said thoughtfully. "And not me either, I don't think. Well maybe me, sort of. But I don't think it's a person really. I think it's your fantasy. You want me to be with Scott. Sexually and romantically. You hate it too, but it turns you on too much to stop. You see? You're a bottom to your cuckold fantasy."

"You've thought a lot about this," I said.

"I told you I read *Literotica* and *ourhotwives*," Jen said. "I'm trying to understand you better. Get inside your head. So I can make it better for you. Make the game better for you."

I nodded slowly, processing all this. We were silent for long moments. Finally, I asked, "So what do we do now?"

"We go home," Jen said. "We go to sleep."

"Sleep?" I asked. I thought, no sex?

Jen read my mind and grinned at me. She said, "It's Friday baby. So we're just platonic roommates."

"What about the Sapphire launch?" I said, shocked.

"I celebrated with you Mike," she said. "But you know the rule. Fridays and Saturdays belong to Scott."

In the uber home, I finally got a chance to tell Jen about the Sapphire launch. I told her how Anderson Cooper and Jasmine Kelly talked about Sapphire on their shows. Jen was really excited and asked me lots of questions. But she kept a respectful distance from me on the car seat and wouldn't hold my hand or let me touch her, other than in friendly platonic ways.

At home, Jen went inside the bathroom and closed the door to undress and get ready for bed. When she came out, she was wearing PJ's that covered her entire body except for her hands and feet.

"This is ridiculous Jen," I said irritably. "Okay, I get it, we won't have sex. But I can't see your body? I can't hug you or even hold your hand?"

Jen paced the room, clearly agitated. "This is hard on me too Mike," she said.

"Don't you see Scott's trying to wedge us apart?" I said with exasperation.

"No Mike. He's helping us explore our fantasies," she said.

I glared at her. It drove me crazy the way she *always* took his side!

"At least we get to sleep in the same bed," she said, as if that made up for everything.

"But I can't hold you," I said. "Was that Scott's idea too?"

Jen nodded. "He doesn't want me to feel like I'm married. He wants me to really feel like I'm his girlfriend," she said. She quickly added, "Just on Fridays and Saturdays."

"This is fucked up Jen," I said angrily. I got into bed and turned away from her.

There was a cold silence between us. Then Jen softly said, "I don't see why you can't ask me questions. About me and Scott."

"Wouldn't that violate some rule?" I spat out bitterly.

"I'd tell Allie, if she asked," she said with a shrug. "You're a better friend than Allie so of course I'll answer any questions you ask."

I rolled around to face her. "Okay," I said, bitterness still in my voice. "Did you fuck Scott tonight?"

"No," she said. "I promised you can watch us. I'm trying to keep my promises, Mike." She was talking about me watching the first time Scott fucked her bareback.

"So he came in your mouth?" I asked.

"Yes."

"You swallowed it?"

"Yes."

"You always swallow it?"

"Yes. I always swallow you too, you know. Except when you want to cum on my face."

"Does Scott ever want to cum on your face?"

"Sometimes."

"Do you let him?"

"Yes."

I was breathing hard now and my cock was rock hard. "Would it break a rule if I played with myself?" I asked.

"I think it's okay, as long as you don't try to touch me," Jen said.

"Does he taste different from me?" I asked as I pushed a hand into my boxers and began stroking myself.

"Yes. He's more musky. You're more sweet."

"So he tastes more manly than me," I said sarcastically.

"I never said that Mike," she said.

"Does he fuck you better than me?" I asked.

Jen hesitated, but she remembered our rule: the truth always, and no sugar coating it. "Yes," she said.

"Is that when you feel love for him? When he makes you cum?"

"I guess."

"What do you mean you guess?"

"It's hard to describe Mike. I feel love for Scotty but it's hard to say exactly when."

"Well, did you feel love for Scott when you had his dick in your mouth tonight?" I asked sarcastically.

Jen didn't answer at first. Then she said, "Mike don't be a shit okay? We both agreed to play. It's not just me. This is *our* game, not just *my* game."

We were both silent. I was mad and hurt, but my cock was still rock hard and I was slowly stroking myself. I said, "Do you love me? Or is it breaking a rule to ask that?"

"Of course, I love you Mike," she said with some exasperation.

"So do you feel that way with Scott?" I pressed. "I'm just trying to understand."

"It feels ... different with Scott," she stammered. Then she said "Can I tell you what I think?"

"Okay," I said warily.

"I think you *want* me to fall in love with Scott. Right?" she gently asked.

I didn't answer for a long time. I knew the answer. But I was afraid to say. Finally, I told the truth. "Yes," I admitted. "And no. I don't know for sure. It scares me."

"But it gets you hot right?" she asked.

"Yes," I said. "Why do you want to know?"

"Because sometimes things come out," she said. "I don't want you to freak if you hear me say something."

"You mean if you say you love him?" I asked.

"Yes."

"Have you said it?"

"No. But I've almost said it," Jen admitted.

"Has he said it?"

"No. But Scotty's the kind of man who won't say it until I say it. And Mike ... it might not be something I say. It might be something you see. Something you see me do. I don't want you to freak."

I stared at her. I was breathing hard, practically panting. Then I closed my eyes and rolled my head back, and I moaned as I came in my boxers.

———————⚬———————

Mike and Jen's Story Continues In
Faithful Wife's Fall From Grace
Book 3
Available at Amazon Kindle and Smashwords.

Don't miss out!

Visit the website below and you can sign up to receive emails whenever Pete Andrews publishes a new book. There's no charge and no obligation.

https://books2read.com/r/B-A-KWSAB-WSTOC

BOOKS 2 READ

Connecting independent readers to independent writers.

Milton Keynes UK
Ingram Content Group UK Ltd.
UKHW010640120124
435917UK00001B/60